ELIZABETH "LIZ" WILLIAMS

THE OTHER SIDE OF THE BED

LOVING SOMEONE WHO SLEEPS NEXT TO ANOTHER

Published by XquisiteNaturally Publishing

(Self-published via Amazon KDP)

ISBN (Paperback): 979-8-9940091-0-9

ISBN (eBook): (To be assigned)

Cover design by Markee Books

Interior design by Elizabeth "Liz" Williams

Author Website: www.XquisiteNaturallyHairCare.com

Instagram: @Lizlovinglife_1978 · @XquisiteVybzLLC · @XquisiteNaturallyHairCareLLC

This book was professionally typeset on Reedsy.

Learn more at reedsy.com

Printed in the United States of America.

First Edition.

First edition

ISBN: 979-8-9940091-0-9

This book was professionally typeset on Reedsy.
Find out more at reedsy.com

For every soul who has ever loved deeply while living in the shadows of someone else's bed. This book is for those who gave their all, questioned their worth, and still found the courage to choose themselves. You are not alone.

"The worst way to miss someone
is when they're standing right beside you—
and you know you can never have them."
— Anonymous

Contents

Foreword

A good friend once asked me to read her manuscript before anyone else, and as I turned the pages, I felt a quiet shift in how I understood love, loyalty, and self-respect. This isn't a dramatic confession meant to provoke or sensationalize. It's the kind of truth you reach for in the middle of the night when the world feels a little too loud and the heart, stubbornly, won't stop asking questions.

Elizabeth "Liz" Williams writes as someone who has stood at the edge of the bed with you—not to judge, but to bear witness. She speaks from years of hard-won experience, from the moment she realized that love can arrive loud and beautiful and still be at odds with the life you're trying to live. She knows what it is to give yourself fully, to be the soft place someone leans on, only to discover that a vow or a story around it can complicate what you deserve most: your own clarity and peace.

This book isn't a pity party. It's a memoir, a mirror, a moment of truth. It names the ache of loving in hiding and refuses to pretend that love alone rewrites the rules. It offers something steadier: a path to choosing yourself with intention, compassion, and courage. It asks us to look inward, to ask what we owe to our own hearts, and to consider what it means to live with honesty when the stakes are high and the consequences real.

To my friend: thank you for writing honestly, for laying out the hard parts without flinching, and for inviting us to walk this road with you. May your words provide not judgment but a steady hand for anyone who has felt the pull between desire and truth.

And to every reader who's ever felt they were the "other person" in a story that doesn't fit the traditional ending: you are not alone. This book stands with you, offering a clearer map: determine what you need, set your boundaries, and learn to love yourself enough to act on that truth.

With warmth and unwavering belief in your journey,

RL

Preface

This book was never meant to be a book. It started as late-night notes on my phone, quiet prayers, and letters I never sent. Words that held pieces of me I wasn't ready to say out loud. But healing has a way of demanding its own stage.

The Other Side of the Bed: Loving Someone Who Sleeps Next to Another was born out of truth—uncomfortable, unfiltered, unashamed truth. It's about love that lingers long after it should have ended, about hope that overstays its welcome, and the power that comes when a woman finally chooses herself.

I wrote this not to relive the pain, but to release it. To remind anyone standing at the crossroads of heartbreak and healing that they are not alone. Every page, every confession, every lesson here is proof that beauty can rise from broken places.

To every woman who's ever loved deeply, stayed too long, or silenced her own voice just to keep the peace—this is for you. May you find the courage to choose yourself, the grace to forgive, and the strength to walk away when love no longer feels like home.

With love and light,
Elizabeth "Liz" Williams

Acknowledgments

First and always, to my sissy poo — my sister, my mirror, and my voice of reason. Thank you for always seeing me, even when I couldn't see myself. Your gift of honesty, love, and intuition has carried me through storms I didn't think I'd survive. I love you endlessly.

To my children, Dominic and Taliya — you are my heartbeat and my forever inspiration. Everything I do, I do with you in mind. Your love reminds me daily of why I fight, why I dream, and why I rise again and again. This book is as much yours as it is mine.

And to everyone who poured into me with encouragement, patience, and understanding — thank you. This journey would not have been possible without your light.

May these pages remind you to always choose yourself.

Prologue

The worst way to miss someone is when they are standing right beside you. They laugh at your jokes, hold your hand when no one's watching, and whisper things in your ear that sound like forever, but they don't stay. They can't. Or they won't. Either way, you're left holding pieces of promises made in silence.

When I met Malik Carter, I wasn't looking for love. I wasn't even looking for attention. My relationship with Stephen — the father of my children — was still standing, but the foundation had already crumbled. We were two people living in the same space, separated by silence and betrayal. His body was present, but his loyalty had long left the room.

Then he appeared charming, attentive, broken in a way I recognized. We met while applying for the same job. It started as a friendship, the kind where you talk for hours about everything and nothing, where you don't realize how much time has passed because, for the first time in a long time, someone actually sees you.

He made me laugh. He challenged me. He called me out on my bullshit, and I appreciated it. Everyone called him MC. I called him Malik. He called me "Nia Morgan, CEO of Everything." We had inside jokes, playlists, matching cups at work... and still, he went home to someone else.

I know what you're thinking: why didn't I walk away? I asked myself the same thing. A thousand times. But love is tricky. It doesn't follow logic, rules, or vows. Love will have you memorizing a man's schedule, not because you're trying to be sneaky, but because you're trying to squeeze into the few moments when he's just yours.

He once told me, "If we had met at another time, you'd be my wife." I used to cling to that sentence like a lifeline, like I was the missed blessing, like I was next in line. But in truth, that sentence is just a polite way of saying, "You'll never be first."

And still I stayed. I stayed when he cried. I stayed when he told me his marriage felt like a prison. I stayed because I thought being his peace would earn me a place in his future.

But peace doesn't beg to be chosen. Peace doesn't settle for scraps. And eventually, neither did I.

Introduction

Imagine the love of your life telling you they're in love with you. They believe you are soulmates. They say all the right things. They know your heart and speak to your spirit. You finish each other's sentences. You dream together. Yet every night, you go home to sleep in your bed alone—and they continue to sleep in their bed with their spouse.

Confusing? It shouldn't be. Not once the love-blinders are removed. (Though I'll admit, taking them off isn't easy.) The truth is, there's only one person truly in love in this situation—and it's not the one sleeping beside someone else every night.

Let me introduce myself. I'm Nia Morgan. I'm not speaking as a victim or a naive woman who was tricked. I'm speaking from experience. Over 20 years of it. I wore my love-blinders with pride, thinking my love would win. I thought that if I gave him all of me—if I proved that he wasn't alone, that he had a partner in me, that I could be the soft place he craved—he would eventually choose me. I was wrong.

And if you've ever been the "other woman" (even if it didn't start that way), you've probably heard this one: "I made a vow to God. I can't go against that." But here's what I eventually learned: if that vow was really guiding him, we wouldn't exist. You and I—the outsiders—we only exist because that vow was already broken long before we showed up.

This is not a pity party. This is a memoir. A mirror. A moment of truth. For every woman who thought love was enough. For every heart that loved fiercely, only to be loved in hiding. This is the other side of the bed.

Let's begin.

1

THE MEET

Florida, 2001

I had just moved from New York to Florida—running more than relocating. I told everyone it was for a fresh start, but truthfully, I was trying to breathe again. Trying to outrun the pieces of my life that didn't fit anymore. Trying to figure out who I was outside of the person I thought I'd spend forever with.

Even though Stephen and I were on a break, my heart hadn't gotten that memo. Love doesn't clock out just because circumstances do. He was still in my bones. Still the future I pictured. Florida may have been new, but I didn't come looking for a new love—just peace.

"You ready for your interview?" my mother asked.

"Yeah, I'm ready. Where's Reggie? He supposed to take me?"

"Reggie, you ready?" she yelled.

"Just come on, fat pig—I'm ready," he called back.

"You know I'm gonna get the job, right?" I teased.

"We shall see."

"Whatever, Reggie. You're a hater. You know you'd love it if your big sis worked with you."

Truth is, my stomach was doing somersaults. Florida heat was one thing—but stepping into a new life was a different kind of hot. Standing there in sandals I thought were cute until that southern humidity disrespected me, I inhaled the heavy air and whispered to myself:

Here goes nothing.

I sat down next to this guy, and all I could think was, Lord, why do those braids look like they're fighting for their life? His scalp was begging for mercy. He had a country drawl and this too-confident posture like life never scared him.

"You been here before?" I asked.

"Yeah, trying to get rehired," he said.

"Oh, okay. What's your name?"

"MC."

"MC? Is that the name your mama gave you?"

He smirked. "Nah. It's Malik Carter."

"I'm Nia Morgan—but you can call me Nia."

We both got hired and ended up in the same training class. Next thing you know, we're glued to each other's hip like Velcro. Malik was four years younger, goofy, charming in a reckless-little-brother way. The type who made boring days feel lighter. I always vibed better with men anyway. Women saw competition; men saw comfort.

He talked freely—about is girlfriend, his little princess. And every time he mentioned them, I mentioned Stephen. Because back then, even broken, Stephen was still him. I wasn't looking to replace what I still prayed would return healed.

One afternoon he said, "Hey Nia, I think I'm gonna shoot my shot at Dez."

"Who?"

"The Supervisor."

"Oh. Well, go ahead and get yourself fired," I said.

"She keep giving me looks. I think she want me."

"You so damn conceited. Go on then. I tried to warn you."

And just like the walking red flag he was, he did. And just like I predicted, it got messy. She caught feelings, he caught convenience, and I caught her watching me like I was the problem.

One day during break, my legs were casually on Malik's lap—no romance, just comfort—and she marched over with a tight jaw.

"That's not professional, Nia," she said. "You shouldn't have your legs on him."

I slid my legs down slow. "Okay," I said sweetly.

Professional? Girl, be serious.

Malik cut her off soon after—said she was too clingy. She kept it "professional" — if you count tight smiles, unnecessary critiques, and staring holes through me in the break room as professional. She never said my name wrong or raised her voice. She weaponized silence, looks, and fake-polite shade instead.

The funny thing is... I wasn't even thinking about Malik like that. My heart was still wrapped around a man hundreds of miles away. But Dez didn't know my heart — she just saw my presence.

At some point, he asked me to braid his hair, and I said yes. Took three days— his head big as his mouth. One night we took a break and sat at a quiet park, on separate benches, silence hanging between us. Not romantic, just... peaceful. Familiar in a way I couldn't explain. But still, it wasn't that. Not to me.

Then one day, in the middle of lunch, he blurted out:

"Nia, would you fuck me?"

If water had been in my mouth, every soul in that break room would've needed towels.

I looked at him like, Sir... be for real.

But I didn't want to hurt him, so I mumbled, "Yeah... sure," while mentally scrolling past that nonsense. He was my homie. A headache, but mine.

He'd brag about the women he entertained. I'd shake my head and remind him of his girl and his daughter. He'd shrug. I'd bring up Stephen. We were both pretending we weren't tied to things we couldn't let go of.

A few weeks later, he got fired. Dez called him to the back. The door didn't slam, but it felt like the whole room held its breath. Five minutes later, Malik walked out, jaw tight, eyes low, grabbing his things without a word.

Dez didn't say much. Just shook her head like, "I gave you a chance, bro."

And just like that, he was gone. Silence settled where he used to sit, and it was louder than he ever was. Sometimes he popped back in or texted something stupid just to annoy me. I never knew when he'd show up, but when he did, I'd smile. Not in love—just in familiarity. In comfort. In knowing someone saw me before Florida did.

Then one day, I got a text message.

MC got arrested.

No details. No explanation. Just a sentence that felt like a slammed door.

I didn't reply. What could I say? Life was already reshaping itself, and we were drifting into separate currents.

Time passed. I moved forward. Grew. Changed. But every now and then, he floated across my memory—the too-tight braids, the silly grin, the way he made my new world less foreign.

"You cool as hell, Nia," he once told me. "You ain't like the rest of these chicks."

Not the sweetest compliment, but I knew what he meant.

With him, I could just be me. No pretending. No proving. Just existing.

And I didn't know it then, but that would matter more than I ever imagined.

2

Reflection 1.5

Liz's Real Thoughts

I decided to add these reflections to give you a little more transparency. The chapters tell the story, but these reflections? They're where I share what I was really feeling and experiencing during those moments in my life. Yes, my name is Liz, but for privacy reasons I'm still using the character names from the book. Your girl is an open book though — if sharing my truth helps somebody else heal, then it's worth it.

Back in those early days, I used to think about Stephen constantly. We talked all the time — long Zoom calls, random check-ins, deep laughs. I missed him. I missed our friendship. And even today, because we share Dante and Tiana, he'll always be in my life — but strictly as an excellent co-parent. Nothing beyond that.

But at that point in my life, newly in Florida, my emotions and attention were wrapped up in Stephen. So looking at Malik in any romantic way? That wasn't even a thought.

But Malik... he was a breath of fresh air.

Easygoing. Funny. Unbothered.

He didn't try hard — and I loved that. Talking to him felt natural. Even with the age gap, the conversation just flowed. It wasn't deep yet, but it was light, comfortable, and exactly what I didn't realize I needed at that time.

I hope you enjoy these reflections — the truth behind the chapters. Tell me what you think when you see me at a reading or signing.

Peace,

Liz

3

TWO YEARS LATER

Two years later felt like a lifetime. Florida wasn't just palm trees and heat anymore—it was home.

Stephen and I had actually tried to really build something here. When he moved down, it felt like a sign. Like maybe all the uncertainty, all the breaks and make-ups finally had a place to land. We had Dante, and for a moment life felt stable—simple in a way my heart didn't always know how to accept.

I was somebody's mother now. Somebody's partner. Somebody building a life that looked right on paper, even if some days I still felt like I was stitching myself together one emotion at a time.

But life has a funny way of circling back to unfinished chapters...

"Where's my phone?"

Ring.

"Hello?"

"Hey, fat pig, what are you doing?"

"Nothing, Reggie, just chilling with Dante. Why, what's up?"

"You won't believe who I ran into at the barbershop."

"Okay, well, damn, spit it out."

"Malik."

"WHAAAAT? Malik? From Unity Solutions?"

"Yup. Gave him your number. He gave me his, too."

I'd never dialed a number so damn fast in my life.

I used to think about him from time to time, wondering what happened with that jail situation, or just how he was doing. But nobody I talked to had heard from him, so I chalked it up to one of those "he was just a co-worker I lost touch with" things.

Nia: "Hello?"

Malik: "Damn, Nia. Omg, how have you been?"

He laughed. "I've been good. You?"

"I'm good. Just had my son, Dante, not too long ago."

"Wow, Nia has a child."

"I know, can you believe it? But that's my Baby D."

"Omg, I gotta see you."

"In due time."

"What? Boy, don't make me bite you. I haven't seen or spoken to you in two years, and you hit me with 'in due time'?"

"Nia, okay, okay."

Later that day:

Malik: "Hey, what are you doing?"

"Leaving Walmart, why?"

"Oh, you're right around where I live. Pass through."

"Okay, cool."

OMG. That's all I could say when I saw this man walk down those stairs.

(Yes, I said man. Malik had grown up, y'all. Lol.)

We hugged each other so tight.

"Wow, Nia, you look good."

"So do you. What have you been up to?"

"Well, after Unity, I got into the cleaning service business. Was doing really good until I lost it all."

"How did that happen?"

"I went into business with a friend. He started slacking, and I ended up losing my life savings, $16,000."

"I'm sorry, did you say $16,000?"

"Yeah."

"Damn, that's a lot of money. I'm really sorry to hear that."

"How's your girlfriend?"

"Well, girlfriend is now wife. She's good."

"Wow. Malik got married?"

"Yeah. It was time. I made an honest woman out of her, and my mom kept asking when

I was gonna marry her, so we just went to the courthouse and did it."

"Well, that's cool."

For some strange reason, him saying he was married made my stomach sink. But I kindly ignored that feeling.

We chatted for a couple more hours, then I left.

Later that evening:

Nia: "Hello?"

Malik: "Hey, you."

"What's up?"

"Nothing. Just here with Dante, cooking. What about you?"

"Damn, Nia. You really looked good earlier."

(Blushing) "Thank you, Malik."

"I wanted to ask you something."

"Okay, shoot."

"You ever think about that time in the park when you were doing my hair?"

"What about it?"

"I wanted to say something to you back then, but I didn't know how."

"Are you serious?"

"Yeah. Not Malik shy, right?"

"I remember when you asked me to fuck at Unity. I was so damn shocked. But I said yes just not to hurt your feelings, since we were friends."

"I always thought you were cool, but I was immature. Plus, I was a male ho."

"Yeah, you were. Lol."

"But I've calmed down. After I got married, Leah's the only woman I'm sleeping with."

"I'm proud of you."

Then I paused, letting my thoughts float out before saying, "All I know is... when I saw you walk down those stairs I was like, "Damn, that's Malik!"

He didn't respond right away. I could hear his breath in the silence.

And in that quiet moment, I knew something had shifted.

Maybe not enough to change the past, but just enough to complicate the present.

4

IN TOO DEEP

It started small, harmless even. Malik didn't have a car for a while, and since we lived close by, I offered to pick him up in the mornings. We didn't work at the same place, but the timing worked out. I'd swing by, he'd hop in, and we'd talk the whole way there like no time had ever passed. He'd drop me off at my job, take the car, and then head to his.

At the end of the day, we'd do the whole thing in reverse. It became our thing.

And then came the outings.

There was a new place that had just opened nearby, and we started going there all the time. It became our unofficial morning hangout. We'd grab food, sit in the car, laugh, and people-watch sometimes for so long, we ended up skipping work entirely. Not often. But enough to make us wonder how we even got paid. Some days we'd walk around the mall. Other times, we'd catch a morning movie and chill the entire day like the world didn't exist. Like we weren't wrapped up in other lives. Other commitments.

There was one day I'll never forget, We were walking past a photography kiosk in the mall. The lady working the booth looked up, smiled, and said, "Aww, y'all are such a cute couple! You should take a picture."

And just like that, without even thinking, we did.

We posed. We smiled. Malik wrapped his arm around me, and I leaned into him like it was the most natural thing in the world. For those few seconds, we weren't "just friends." We weren't caught up in complicated situations. We were just... us.

The flash went off, and that's when it hit.

We both snapped out of it, looked at each other, and said in perfect unison, "Oh no, wait, delete that photo!"

The lady laughed, thinking we were joking. But we weren't. We had both completely forgotten that we were in other relationships. That moment was real in a way it wasn't supposed to be. That photo would've captured more than just our smiles.

It would've captured the truth we weren't ready to face.

And then... came the kiss.

There was a time when Malik told me his wife said he didn't know how to kiss. And me, being his naive best-friend sidekick, I was like, Oh, I'll teach you. I'm a great kisser.

Anyway, one day he had to go to his apartment for something (I don't remember what.)

He checked the mail and turned to me, saying, "I thought you said you were going to teach me how to kiss."

I said, "Yeah, sure. No problem."

Then he pushed me up against the wall, and I was like, "Okay, hold on, pause."

I told him, "Show me how you kiss. I'm not going to move, but I want you to show me what you do."

And oh my God...it was like kissing a wet fish. He kissed everywhere. Mouth juice all over my face. Yeah, no. That wasn't right at all.

I had to stop him. "Okay, hold on," I said. "I'm going to kiss you. I'm going to show you what I do with my lips and tongue, but I don't want you to move. Just feel what I'm doing."

He agreed.

I did.

Then I asked, "So, did you feel it?"

He said, "Yes."

"All right. Now I want you to do the same thing back to me."

So we practiced back and forth for a bit, and I thought, Oh shit. I think we're in trouble.

But anyway, the report that got back to me? He said, "Wow... my wife said I kiss so much better now."

And in my head, I was like, How the hell is she not wondering where you got that from?

— -

Around that same time, things between Stephen and me had started to crumble. He had stepped out on our relationship, and no matter how hard I tried, something in me shut down. I didn't want to be intimate with him anymore. The connection felt forced—like we were trying to hold on to a version of "us" that no longer existed.

Eventually, we agreed to make our relationship open. It wasn't something I ever thought I'd do, but it felt like the only way to breathe again. We set rules—boundaries that were supposed to keep the peace. Stephen could entertain others, and I could go out, too. But let's be real—there was no way he was going to step out on me and I not have my fun as well.

One day while I was at work, I called Malik.

"Hey Malik, I have a question," I said.

He laughed a little, like he already knew it was going to be something wild. "What's up, Nia?"

I explained everything—how Stephen and I decided to open things up, how I wasn't trying to play games or be reckless, but I needed someone I trusted. Someone who understood discretion. Someone who knew me.

Then I asked, "Would you be that person for me?"

There was a long pause on the other end of the line.

Finally, Malik said softly, "Nia... I can't. I'm married."

His words hit a little harder than I expected. I felt hollow for a moment—but I understood. I really did. I respected it.

The next morning, my phone rang. It was Malik.

"You still serious about what you said?" he asked.

"Yes," I said, without hesitation. "I know with you it'll just be us comforting each other, and my business won't be all over Florida."

He was quiet again, for a few seconds that felt like forever. Then he exhaled and said, "Okay, Nia... yes. I'll comfort you."

And just like that, I was cheesing like a schoolgirl—grinning at my phone like the trouble had already begun.

5

Reflection 4.5 - The Line We Pretended Didn't Exist

At that time in my life, riding to work with Malik felt like a breath of fresh air. It was a break from my usual routine of driving alone after dropping Dante off at daycare. Having someone to laugh with, talk to, and even discover new breakfast spots with made my mornings lighter. It was simple, innocent... but also more than either of us wanted to admit back then.

Looking back now, after writing this book, it's obvious — there were feelings there. Real ones. But we were both too afraid, too loyal, too unsure to call them what they were. So we just kept them tucked away, pretending friendship was the whole story.

What still blows my mind is how strangers could see what we were trying to hide. We'd be in Walmart, just shopping, and this older lady walked straight up to us and said, "I just want to tell you two... y'all are really in love." And Malik, being Malik, smiled and said, "Yes, we are." I would laugh it off, but inside I'd be thinking, Why do random people keep saying this? What are they seeing that we're trying so hard to ignore?

They saw something real — something we weren't brave enough to acknowledge yet.

Meanwhile, things with Stephen were falling apart. I didn't trust him anymore. He stepped out on our relationship right after Dante was born, and that broke something in me. I kept trying to figure out what I did wrong, what I could fix, how I could make him want us again. When I finally asked him what I wasn't doing or how I could improve, he told me, "You're damn near perfect. I'm just that n**** that's going to cheat."

That response changed me forever. It hardened me. It woke me up. It birthed the version of me who doesn't apologize for prioritizing herself. Back then, I was naïve. I took everything people said at face value because I'm an honest woman who believes in honesty. His words shifted that.

After that, I couldn't be intimate with him anymore. He didn't want to separate, didn't want to divide the home — especially with Dante being so young — but I felt taken advantage of. That's when the idea of an open relationship came up. He wasn't with it at first, even though he had already been living his version of an open relationship without my consent. But I needed freedom too. I needed something for me.

When he finally agreed, I told him my side of "open" was just me going out, having drinks, dancing — which was partly true — but really, I was trying to get him to say yes. Because there was no way he was out having fun, I wasn't sleeping with him, and I also wasn't allowed to experience anything for myself. That wasn't happening.

So I called Malik with the proposition. And when he declined, my feelings were hurt. Bad. But I'm good at hiding how I feel until I'm ready to share it. I accepted it on the surface, but inside... it stung.

Then the next day, he called back and said yes.

And that changed everything.

I was shocked... but also relieved. Happy. Because your girl was pent up, and I needed some TLC too. And at that time, I wasn't thinking about his marriage the way I probably should have. He had already shared the issues he was having at home, and in my mind, I thought it would never go past our friendship — just two people fulfilling a need and keeping it moving.

At least, that's what I told myself.

I hope you all are enjoying these Reflections after the chapters.
— Liz

6

ANIMAL MAGNETISM

September 18, 2008

Stephen and I had decided to give things another try. We weren't perfect—far from it—but we agreed that love deserved one more shot. He had just started a new trucking job and was gone more than he was home, but it was supposed to help us build something real. Stability. A future. That's what I told myself, anyway.

The timing couldn't have been worse. We were in the middle of moving, surrounded by boxes and half-packed memories. Between Stephen's schedule and Rhea's mouth, I felt like I was doing everything alone. That's when Malik showed up again—steady, familiar, too damn close for comfort.

"Happy birthday, old man. So how you feeling?" I asked, sliding into the driver's seat.

He smirked, that lazy grin that always made my stomach flip.
    "It's just another day. You see I'm about to help you pack."

"Well, Rhea and Mommy are at the house, packing up some stuff, so I'm going to take you out for a birthday breakfast."

Just him sitting in my car had me on fire. I didn't know how much longer I could play this cat-and-mouse game we'd been tangled in.

"So, you ever ate here before?"

"Nah. You?"

"Me neither. Mommy was telling me about this pancake house. Hope the food's good."

"Me too, knowing your picky ass."

"Whatever, old man."

RING!!!!

"Hello? What do you mean by where I'm at? Y'all need me to move a dresser? OK,

Mommy, I'll be there in a minute."

"Let's hurry up. They are acting like they need help for one dresser. And it's two of them!"

"Well happy birthday again, sexy."

"Why are you staring at me like that?"

"This is the sweetest thing anyone has ever done for me."

"Are you serious?"

"Yeah. Thanks, Nia."

"No problem, butt head. Let's go."

— -

"You two got the dresser down by yourselves, didn't need me after all."

"Shut up. What were you doing anyway?"

"We went to breakfast. It's Malik's birthday."

"Hey, Ms. Morgan."

"What's up, Rhea?"

"Hey, Malik," they said in unison. I could tell they both had attitudes. Whatever. They'd get over it.

"Nia, can I talk to you for a minute?" My sister Rhea, even though she's a year younger, always acted like the oldest , stayed in "mommy" mode.

"Yeah, sure. What's up?"

"I'm just gonna speak to you straight."

"Okay."

"He is a married man."

"I know that, Rhea."

"I'd look at you so differently if you slept with this man."

"What are you talking about? He's my best friend. I'm not sleeping with him. He's just helping me move."

"Yeah, okay. I'm your sister. I know you."

"Whatever, Rhea. We're just friends."

And I didn't even believe the words that came out of my own mouth. Lord knows I wanted to feel this man inside me, behind me, all over me. And there wasn't a person on this planet who knew me better than my sister.

"Damn, Nia, you should've seen how he was staring at you while you talked to Rhea like he wanted to eat you alive."

"I hope you two don't think you're fooling anybody. That attraction is thick. Y'all are like animals."

"Mommy, what are you talking about?"
  "Nia, when you two are together, the sexual tension is so obvious. It's like "Oh my God, will these two just do it already?"

Laughing: "Mommy, you're so damn silly."

"Okay, I'll play dumb.
  "Come on, Ma!" , shouted Rhea

"Alright, your impatient daughter is calling. See you later, love you."

—-

"Rhea and Mommy are crazy."
  "Why? What happened?"

"Rhea's like, 'Nia, don't sleep with that man, he's married.' And Mommy's like, 'Just fuck already.'"

"She said that?"

"Yup. She also said the sexual tension is all over the place."

"Damn, babe. Do we tell on ourselves that much?"

"Apparently. We're not fooling those two."

—-

To my surprise, we actually started packing for real, load after load, back and forth to the car. But my feisty ass, being in a room with him? It was starting to take a toll.

"I can't do this anymore."

"Do what?"

"Act like we don't have unfinished business."

"What are you talking about, Nia?"

"Don't make me hurt you, Malik. You still have a lot of packing to do, and I don't know if I can come back here and help."

"Don't worry about it. I'll get help. You're not the only friend I have."
  He laughed, dropped the box, and pushed me up against the wall.

"Damn."

"You sure you're ready?"

"Let me taste you, Malik."

"Hold up... what now?"

"Nothing. Let's just take a shower first."

"Okay... damn. I don't even have a shower curtain. Took that down already. We're going to wet up the floor."

"Okay, so we'll do this another time."

"Don't play with me, get your ass in the damn shower."

I stood there watching him strip. Body sculpted. ass perfect. Just neat and fine in all the right ways.

"Dude, you really need to shave. Wax. Nair. Something."

"What are you talking about?"

"All that damn hair. That's got to go."

We couldn't dry off because the towels were already packed. Next thing I knew, he threw me on the bed. Aggressive. Loved it.

Legs spread wide, he just stared at my pussy like it was his first meal of the day.

"What happened?" I asked.

"It's so clean. No hair."

"Told you I laser. You feel so much cleaner that way."

"You sure you're ready?"

"Boy, don't play with me. You see how wet I am."

He kissed my inner thighs. Took his time. Didn't rush. Licked around my mound like he was savoring me. No one had ever made me feel like that before.

When he finally found my clit, oh my God! I grabbed at the sheets, screamed his name, legs trembling.

He held me down like he owned me.

"Malik! Oh shit, Malik!"

And then he flipped me like I weighed five pounds and took me from behind.

Pounding. Deep. In rhythm, like we were made for each other. My back arched toward his body over mine.

"Damn, babe. Your pussy is so good."

He grunted, hips meeting mine in a perfect storm. Then he whispered

"Ugh... I'm about to cum... ooh shit."

His whole body trembled as he released. Marked me. Claimed me.

I couldn't even tell you when I passed out.

— -

"Hey, babe, wake up."

"Huh?"

"You don't want to finish packing?"

"Packing? Oh my God, when did I fall asleep?"

"Don't laugh. Granny's knocked out. The youngster wore you out."

"Whatever."

"I was actually just watching you sleep."

"You were?"

"Yeah."

"Okay, let's get up and do something."

"Alright, last trip to the car. I'm exhausted."

"Your grandma ass."

"Yeah, okay."

He layed out on the floor as soon as we got back upstairs. I straddled him and kissed him.

"Wow, you kiss way better now."

"Well, I had a great teacher."

"Silly."

"Hey... you want to go again?"
  "Hell yeah, let's go."

7

LOVE IN THE IN-BETWEEN

After that night, Malik and I became intimate, everything changed. There was no more pretending it didn't mean something. We had crossed a line, and neither of us wanted to go back. From that point on, it wasn't just about sneaking glances or sharing inside jokes. It felt like we were in an actual relationship, one with routines, with holidays, with stolen traditions that most people in our situation never got to have.

Somehow, we managed to find each other in the moments people like us usually miss out on. Even the holidays, especially the holidays. While most people juggling commitments would be lucky to get a phone call or a hurried meet-up the day before or after, we somehow always had the day.

Like Valentine's Day.

Dante's father was on the road, driving trucks like he always did, and Malik called me and told me to meet him behind his apartment complex. Not at the main entrance. Not out front. The back, like it...was our little hideaway from the world.

I pulled up, and he was already waiting. He didn't say a word at first, just walked up, pulled me close, and sat me right on the hood of my car, like it was the most natural thing in the world. We didn't go out, didn't have some fancy dinner or big display. We just sat there, legs swinging, talking, laughing, vibing like we were the only two people alive.

And that was the beauty of it, February 14th, the actual day. Not the 13th. Not the 15th. The day. It meant something. It meant everything. Because so many people who find themselves in what we had don't get that kind of time, they got leftovers. We got the main course.

And then came my birthday.

He was supposed to be watching the match with his friends, it was some big-deal play-off or championship night. I remember texting him earlier, just joking around, saying, "Don't forget to tell me happy birthday before the game has you hypnotized."

He texted back:

"I've got you. Actually, you've got me. I'm pulling up."

I didn't expect him to actually come. But about an hour later, there he was, knocking at the door with a bottle of wine, pizza, and a smirk.

We curled up in bed, talking like we always did. Somewhere between the second glass and the second round of jokes, I told him a story that had him in stitches.

I was like, "You know, a stripper once made me climax five times on my 21st birthday."

He sat up so fast, like I'd just challenged his manhood outright. "Five? Nah, that's mad. All right. Bet."

He went into full-on "Birthday Challenge" mode. I swear, this man turned it into an Olympic event, stretching, psyching himself up, even slapping his own hands together like he was about to dunk. I couldn't stop laughing.

"Don't gas yourself," I teased.

"Oh no, now I've got to beat that. You're talking records, I'm trying to make history."

And let me tell you something, I don't remember if he actually hit five, but I do remember my legs gave out before he did. Between the effort, the jokes, the playful trash talk, and how seriously he took it... that night was more than just sex. It was one of those rare moments where pleasure, love, and pure joy collided.

Afterwards, we laid there, tangled up, breathless and giggling. My body was tired, my heart was full.

"I should have left the game eons ago," he mumbled, pulling me closer. "Yeah," I whispered. "You definitely won this birthday."

And it wasn't just about that night. It was the fact that he chose to be there on the days that mattered. Birthdays. Holidays. The days most people in our position have to sacrifice or explain away. We didn't. Somehow, we made it work. And every time...

Every time we did, it stitched us a little closer together.

The love we shared grew quietly, steadily, yet undeniably. And though we both knew deep down that it was temporary, something fragile living in the cracks of two separate lives, we still lived in it fully.

It was messy.

It wasn't very easy.

But it was ours.

8

Reflection 7.5 — When Leaving Was the Only Way to Stay Whole

The decision to bring another beautiful life into the world with Stephen was mine. Before Dante, he already had children, so he wasn't exactly excited about having more. But I knew what I wanted for my life: one father for my children, one home, one family unit. When I explained that to him, he agreed. And that's how my mini-me, Tiana, was created.

But around that time, something shifted between Malik and me.

We had always felt something for each other — something quiet, something unspoken, something deep. But now, those feelings were rising to the surface in a way we could no longer hide. And once Malik finally got his own car and didn't need to ride with me to work anymore, a little space formed between us. It wasn't intentional. It just... happened. But even in that space, we were still doing the things couples do — holidays, conversations, planning our days around each other. Most people in a situation like ours never get moments like that, but somehow we did.

Funny enough, a year before I got pregnant with Tiana, he'd had his youngest daughter. And when I got pregnant, that's when the real distance came. I get it — I'm not a man, but I understand. The woman who has your heart is pregnant... and it's not your child. That has to feel like something.

And me? My crazy self didn't care. If we're being honest, I still wanted him. I still loved being near him. But even with the space between us, we were still making time for each other, still trying to figure out whatever it was we thought we could balance.

Let me explain something about me:
   I'm territorial.
   If I consider you mine — my man, my lover, my person — then that's exactly what it is. Labels or not.

So when I saw Malik with his family one day — all of them getting into their car looking happy, and him wearing his "family face" — something snapped inside me. Not anger. Not jealousy. Just truth.

Seeing him living two different lives hurt.
   Seeing him in a version of his world that I wasn't included in hurt even more.

I realized I only had two options:

1. Act a fool
   or
2. Leave Florida before I lost myself

And deep down, I knew I had to go.

I couldn't keep running into them in the neighborhood. I couldn't keep pretending it didn't bother me. I couldn't keep risking being the friend — the woman — that disrupted someone else's home. I loved him, but I loved myself too. And I could feel my mask slipping. Eventually, the truth was going to come out in ways I wouldn't be able to control.

So I went home that night and talked to Stephen. He had brought up moving to Texas several times before, but I always said no — because of Malik. Because of whatever Malik and I were, or weren't, or could have been.

But that night? I was done fighting what I knew I needed.

I looked at Stephen and asked,
   "Do you still want to move to Texas?"

He didn't hesitate. "Hell yeah."

"Well," I said, "let's do it."

His face told me he couldn't believe I meant it. But I did.

We went to Trinidad Carnival in February, lived our best lives one last time, and by March we packed up the kids, said our goodbyes, had our farewell dinners, and we were out.

And Malik?
   He didn't take it well at all.

He ghosted me.
   Got upset.
   Told me he couldn't believe I just left him.

Mind you — this man was married — but I was the one who "left him."
   The math wasn't mathing, but the emotions were real.

Even after the move, that first year in Texas broke me in ways I didn't expect. I was raising two kids, adjusting to a new state, no family support, no friends, no familiar anything. And on top of that, Malik barely spoke to me.

The texts I sent...
   The calls I made...
   The way he would answer short, or hang up when he felt overwhelmed...

He didn't move like I moved — with that all-in, heart-open loyalty. And that caused fractures between us that never fully healed.

But at the end of the day, I had to do what was best for me.
   For my children.
   For my peace.
   And as much as I loved Malik, I never wanted to be the woman who disrupted his home or destroyed his family. He was my best friend first. And sometimes loving someone means stepping away before you become the storm that breaks everything.

This was my truth.
   This was the shift.
   This was the beginning of letting go.

— Liz

9

MINE, BUT NOT MINE

The love between Malik and I? It was magnetic. Deep. Almost dangerous. The kind of connection that could bend time, years slipping away without either of us realizing how long we'd been living two lives.

His. Mine. And ours.

Somewhere in the midst of it all, I enrolled in cosmetology school. I'd always loved doing hair, making women feel beautiful, transforming someone's confidence with just a touch.

Malik supported me, like he always did. It became part of our rhythm: he'd pick me up in the mornings, drop me at school, then head to work. Sometimes we'd ride in silence, sometimes we'd talk about nothing. But even in the quiet, there was always that undercurrent of something too big to name.

We were still going through the motions of our real lives, yet somehow we always carved out space to live our own — for years.

But something inside me began to shift.

See, I'm territorial. If you're mine, then you're mine. All mine. And even though Malik made me feel like he belonged to me, like I had all of him, I knew I didn't. Not truly. He still had a wife. He still had a family, a home I would never enter through the front door, because no matter how much he made me feel like his, I'd never be his all, his wife, his forever.

And after a while, that ache settled in my chest. It wasn't always loud. Some days, I could ignore it. But on other days? It screamed.

We started going to the gym together every morning. That became our new thing: Malik would meet me there, and we'd push each other through every set, every run, every drop of sweat.

He would meet me early, and we'd knock out a workout before school and work. Just the two of us. It became our quiet escape once more.

Until one morning, he hit me with:

"Hey... my wife wants to work out too. Let's just use the gym over at my complex today."

I paused. Stared at the message. Read it again.

My whole spirit tightened. Like, what?!?!?! The gym was our thing. It felt like she was now walking into our sacred space. I caught a full attitude. I didn't even try to hide it. But I didn't argue. I just texted back, "OK," and decided I'd show up and behave for the sake of not blowing up the whole damn secret.

All three of us were in the gym that morning: him, his wife, and me. It was awkward as hell, no matter how calm I pretended to be. Malik, trying to play it cool, was giving us both workout tips, splitting his attention like he wasn't standing between his real life and his secret one. And I was watching every little thing.

Then the baby started crying.

They had just had a baby girl not long ago, and the sound came through the speaker on his wife's phone. She paused mid-exercise and said she needed to check on her. Malik nodded. I pretended not to care.

His wife left to tend to the baby.

A few minutes later, I stood near the mirror and asked, "Wanna just do some cardio? Walk around the complex?"

He hesitated just for a second, then nodded.

We started walking. It was quiet at first, just sneakers on concrete, breathing in sync. By the time we reached the back of the complex, behind the old white van near the maintenance shed, it was like we both knew.

He pulled me to him without a word. We didn't speak. There was no sweet talk, no warm-up, just this raw, desperate need to feel something real.
Just for a few stolen minutes he kissed me like he was mad at himself for wanting me so much, as if trying to memorize me before the world came crashing back in.

And when we were done, we pulled ourselves back together, as if it were nothing.

No trace.
No words.

Just... breath. Guilt. Love. All wrapped up in one moment that neither of us would ever speak aloud.

He walked me back to my car, back to our routines.
Me to school.
Him to work.
Both of us pretended the morning hadn't felt like a gut punch..

That day, I felt it deeply. He was mine, but not mine. And the war between my heart and my reality had only just begun.

10

THE END OF US

My phone rang.

I picked up. "Hello?"

"Hey, Nia."

"What's up, Malik?"

"Nothing. I just left the shop to grab something to eat. I need you to meet me at Brook Haven park today."

"Brook Haven? Why?"

"It's important, Nia. I want to talk to you about something, and I need to say it in person."

Now I was nervous. What was so serious that he couldn't say it over the phone?

"Alright," I said. "Give me a minute. I'll meet you there."

"Don't stop for any burgers, just come straight. It's important."

"Okay, damn. Bye."

He really knew me. I was definitely about to stop for chips, but something in his voice made me change my mind.

I pulled up to the park with my stomach in knots, afraid this might be the moment he told me we had to stop, that it was over.

He looked at me and said, "Took you long enough, Grandma."

"Whatever, Pops. What's this all about?"

"Just walk with me. Be patient. Damn, you New Yorkers are always in a

45

rush."

As we walked, he took my hand. I didn't know what was coming, but I hoped it wasn't goodbye.

We sat on a bench, and when I looked at him, he seemed lighter, like something had been lifted.

"Nia Morgan," he said, "this isn't easy, but I need to say it. These past two years have been the best I've ever had. You're everything I ever wanted. You've made me feel like a man again. I love you. You're my soulmate."

He paused.

"Lena and I talked. We're still together because of the kids, and because neither of us believes in divorce. But that's not the kind of marriage I want. I want to be with someone I can't live without, someone I can grow with. And that person... is you."

Tears ran down my face. I'd waited so long to hear this.

He got down on one knee, took out a ring, and looked me straight in the eyes.

"Nia Morgan, I love you. I don't want to spend another second without you. Will you marry me?"

"Yes. Yes. Yes. Yes!" I kissed him all over his face, crying with joy. "Yes, Malik Carter—I will marry you."

It was perfect.

I was marrying my best friend. It was a beautiful spring day, and I woke from my nap with butterflies.

My mom walked in and smiled. "My baby's getting married today. Come on, it's time to get ready."

My sister Rhea rushed in. "Girl, you're moving too slow. Go shower, we've got hair and makeup to do!"

As I stood up, I smiled. "Can you believe I'm marrying Malik today?"

"Nia, you two are meant to be. Now move your ass." That's my big/little sister.

We got dressed, did my makeup, and slipped me into my gown. Everyone told me I looked beautiful. My mom pinned my veil and hugged me tight.

The limo pulled up, and we arrived at the church.

"You ready?" Rhea asked.

"I'm ready to become Nia Carter."

My dad walked me down the aisle as Jeffrey Osborne's Rest of Our Lives played. Malik stood there in his white tuxedo, looking like a dream.

And that's exactly what it was, a fucking dream.

I woke up.

Living in Texas as a stay-at-home mom had my ass delusional. With Dante at school, Stephen at work, and just baby girl and I at home, no contact from Malik had me spiraling. Back to reality…

Stephen and I had started finding our way back to each other. It wasn't perfect, but it felt familiar—steady in a way I thought I needed. After Dante, I told myself I didn't want to have children with different fathers. So when Stephen and I decided to try again, having Tiana wasn't an accident. It was planned—a conscious choice to build some kind of stability, even if my heart was still split between what was and what could've been.

Malik and I were still close, but not like before. The calls slowed down. The energy shifted. Life was moving, rearranging us both in quiet ways. The love was still there, lingering in the background, but it no longer demanded the same space.

One day, I called Malik…

"Hey, what's up?"

"Malik, I woke up this morning and just… I can't be in Florida anymore."

Silence.

A silence that screamed louder than words.

"Really? Why?"

"Let's stop pretending. You're married, and I'm in love with you so deeply it feels like it's cracking my bones. Every corner, every place here holds a memory of you… and the thought of bumping into you two together?" I swallowed hard. "We're moving to Texas."

He paused, stunned. "Are you serious?"

"Dead serious. Florida's suffocating me."

"When?"

"March. After Trinidad. Stephen's on board."

"Wow... that soon?"

"Yeah. But it's for the best."

A beat of silence passed.

"Alright, Nia, I gotta go. Talk to you later."

"Okay... bye."

Click.

He hung up.

Just like that. I told the man I was uprooting my life... and all I got was "Talk to you later."

I stared at the phone, willing it to ring again.

It didn't. My heart didn't just break, it cracked wide open, and I felt every tremor in my soul.

Days passed. No texts. No calls. Just the loud echo of abandonment.

Then, finally, a message:

Malik: Hey.

Nia: What's up?

Malik: I'm not ignoring your calls. Just caught up with this five-day account. She's been helping me, so she's been around a lot. I want to talk, but I don't have anything nice to say right now. I just need time.

Nia: What do you mean, "don't have anything nice to say"?

Malik: I'm angry, Bae... it's natural. You just left me.

I stared at those words, my fingers trembling.

Nia: You're angry? Do you know what it took for me to walk away? You said you wouldn't even see me before I left. How long were you going to let me just... fade away? A century? A lifetime?

I couldn't believe it. He was mad?

The man who stayed in a marriage he swore was loveless. The man who whispered forever into my skin at night but couldn't even meet me halfway in the daylight.

I was spiraling depressed, snapping at the kids over nothing, still hopelessly in love with a man who belonged to someone else.

I texted again.

Nia: Call me.

And this time... he did.

"Hey. What are you doing?"

"Getting the girls ready for church," he said, his voice soft, too soft for the weight in my chest.

I broke. "I miss you so much. I feel... I feel lost. I don't even know if this move was the right decision."

He paused.

"Nia... what do you want from me?"

I whispered, "I just want to talk. Sometimes. I just want to hear your voice."

Silence again, the kind that makes your ears ring and your heart panic.

"I don't know how to do that," he said, quiet but heavy. "You left me. You were mine... and then you just left."

"I had to. You weren't leaving her. And I was drowning in the in-between."

A beat.

"I'm sorry, babe. But I can't do this. I'm not built like you. I'm in love with you. I'll always love you."

Click.

"Hello?! Malik?!"

But the line was already dead.

And I sat there, cradling the phone like a child who had lost her favorite toy, but it wasn't a toy. It was a man. My man. My love. My ghost.

And I cried. Lord, I cried from a place so deep I hadn't known existed. I wailed for every whispered promise, every stolen moment, every daydream that would never bloom.

That's how it ended.

The saga of Malik and Nia... undone by reality.

I know some of y'all are probably shaking your heads, thinking, That's what she gets. And maybe you're right.

But that doesn't make the pain any less real. Doesn't erase the love. Doesn't patch the hole in my chest.

What I know now is this:

I will never again bleed for a man who won't even bring me a bandage.

I will never again stretch myself thin for someone who won't meet me in the middle.

I will never again make myself available to an unavailable man.

...Or so I thought at the time.

PART 2

THE OTHER SIDE OF THE BED: LOVING SOMEONE WHO SLEEPS NEXT TO ANOTHER

Alright, y'all, did you miss me?

Because whew... It's time.

In Part One, I boldly declared that I would never, and I meant never, make myself available to an emotionally unavailable man again. I stood ten toes down in that truth. I said it with my chest.

And then I did it. Again.

Same man.

Same damn man.

Twelve years later, and somehow here we are. I'm still trying to release someone who was never mines to keep.

So buckle up, grab your wine, clutch your pearls, or whatever you need to get through this because, baby, this ride right here?

It ain't smooth. It ain't safe. And it sure as hell ain't over.

Let's get into it.

11

HERE WE GO AGAIN

Before we get back to Malik, because trust me, that chapter is coming, let me catch y'all up on what life has been like for me these past twelve years.

So picture this: me, two beautiful children, Dante and Tiana and their father, packing up and moving to Houston, Texas. A fresh start... or so I thought.

That first year? Whew. I was going through it. Not just adjusting to a new city, a new life, and full-time motherhood, but also dealing with the fact that Malik was pissed. He cut me off for leaving. No calls, no texts. Just silence. And that silence? It was deafening?

I was a stay-at-home mom, raising Tiana and Dante and trying to hold it all together, but the relationship with their father had already flat lined. We were just two people playing house with no heartbeat left. Eventually, the kiddies and I moved back to Florida, only to boomerang right back to Houston a week later. The relationship with Stephen finally hit its expiration date, and honestly, it had been spoiled for a long time. But that's a messy book I'll save for another time.

Once I was back in Houston for good, I poured myself into what I loved: hair. I rediscovered myself through my craft, enhancing beauty, restoring crowns, and connecting with other Black women who needed to feel seen and celebrated. I officially became a natural hair stylist, and baby, I thrived.

After the breakup with Stephen, I took two full years for myself. No dating, no distractions, just me learning how to be on my own. For the first time in my life, I wasn't answering to anyone. I wasn't shrinking to fit a relationship. I was growing. Healing. Becoming.

Now, fast-forward.

I met someone. Let's call him what he was: a Hobo Lover. One of those men looking for love and a place to stay. That relationship dragged on for five years, and to this day, I honestly think it lasted that long just because he made me laugh. But baby, giggles don't pay bills or build futures.

While I was still working at the salon, I bumped into another man, let's call him Mr. Unknown. This one had his own businesses, swagger, and maturity. A refreshing change after the clingy comedy show I had just left. But he came with his own complications: going through a divorce, not looking for anything serious, and emotionally off-limits. Sound familiar?

We weren't in a relationship, but the situation felt deep. Being around a real man again, one who didn't need me to build him up, was intoxicating. And yet, it drained me too. Loving someone who's halfway healed is still just loving someone who's halfway available.

That connection lasted about four years, and when it fizzled out, I didn't fall apart. I leveled up.

I opened my own salon. My name is on the lease. My hands are in demand. My space, my rules. That was a win I'll never stop being proud of.

Shortly after I moved to Houston, Malik and his family moved to Orlando. Funny how life has a way of keeping us under the same sky, just in different states.

Now fast-forward again. My home girl T, wild, fun, and always ready to party, asked me while I was doing her hair, "Nia, you wanna hit this Reggae Fest with me? It's in Florida."

My birthday was coming up anyway, so I was like, why not? Cool vibes, good music, say less.

But then she said the one word that made my stomach flip.

Orlando.

And y'all already know who lives in Orlando.

Malik.

The moment she said it, my answer turned from "maybe" to "hell yes". I went home, booked my flight and hotel, and didn't even hesitate.

Then... I sent the text.

"Guess who's coming to Orlando?"

He was shocked. Then he called.

His voice? Same deep tone. Same tension. Same everything I'd tried to forget.

So now here we are.

Me, all grown up, fresh off a glow-up, touching down in his city like a storm he never saw coming.

Buckle up.
    Because what happens next?
    Chile, it's about to go down.

12

LIKE WE NEVER LEFT

February 3rd

The day had finally come, the day Malik and I would lay eyes on each other again after all these years. The wait was over, and honestly, it couldn't have played out more perfectly. I landed in Orlando early that morning, and my home girl wasn't set to arrive until later that evening. That gave Malik and me just enough time to reconnect.

But what's wild is we didn't even need the time to get back into sync.

From the moment I touched down, picked up the rental, checked into the Marriott, and settled into that beautiful room, I could feel it. That pull. The nerves. The anticipation. I sat on the bed, heart racing, eyes glued to the door like a scene from a romantic movie.

And then came the knock.

I didn't walk, I damn near flew to that door.

It was still during the COVID shift-back-to-normal era, so when I opened the door and saw him with a mask on, I giggled. But as soon as he pulled me into his arms, baby... whew. That hug wasn't just a "hello." It was an exhale. A "finally." An "I can't believe you're real and right in front of me again." It wasn't awkward, not even a little. No weird pauses, no small talk fillers. Just a seamless slide back into what once was.

We caught up, kicked off our shoes, and spent the next hour talking like time had never passed. He was smaller than I remembered, slimmer, more refined, but still had that same fire in his eyes. I could see something behind them, though. Some weight. And as much as I wanted to dig into it, I didn't want to ruin the moment.

Eventually, we settled on a spot to eat, despite his Virgo brain going into overdrive trying to make sure it was somewhere I'd love. (Yes, I'm particular. I call it standards.) We sat together on the same side of the booth, not across from each other, because being close was a need, not a preference. We ate, laughed, and reminisced. At one point, he fed me a bite of his vegan wrap and wrinkled his nose at mine, but I didn't care. I was glowing from the inside out just being next to him.

Back in the room, we lay on separate beds, pretending like the air between us wasn't crackling with electricity. The truth is, I didn't come to Orlando with any plan to sleep with him. I just needed to see him with my own eyes, to make sure he was okay, to confirm that the connection I felt all these years hadn't just been in my head.

But somewhere in the middle of our conversation, him mid-sentence, me sitting cross-legged on the bed, he leapt over and silenced me with a kiss. Whew. That kiss? Still soft. Still slow. Still his. I teased him, whispering, "You must've had a great teacher," and he smirked into my mouth like he already knew. Before I knew it, my shirt was somewhere on the floor, and Malik... Malik found every curve like he had never forgotten a single one.

He touched me like I was his, like he had something to prove after twelve years apart.

"Damn, Nia," he groaned, mouth trailing down my body. "You still taste like heaven."

And just like that, we collapsed into each other's emotions first, bodies second.

But the weekend wasn't just about lust. T and I had an amazing time at the reggae fest. We danced to old-school Soca and Reggae, throwing it back like we were in our early 20s. The food, the vibe, the music, it was soul medicine. But even as I danced, even with all the laughter and energy, my heart was secretly counting down the hours until

Monday, when I'd be wrapped up in Malik's arms again.

And that last night before my flight? Let's just say we made the most of every second.

THE NIGHT BEFORE THE FLIGHT

T had left on an early morning flight, and I had gladly dropped her off. The day was getting late. My suitcase was half-zipped in the corner, and my boarding pass glowed on my phone screen.

Malik sat behind me on the bed, massaging my shoulders with those warm, steady hands. I leaned back into his chest, eyes closed, not ready to say goodbye.

"You really leaving me again?" he asked, voice low against my neck.

"I don't want to," I said softly.

He turned me around and looked into my eyes like he was searching for a place to stay.

"Then don't," he whispered before kissing me, slow, deliberate, desperate.

We undressed each other like it was sacred. No rush. No games. Just skin, soul, and the gravity that kept pulling us back together.

He laid me down like I was something fragile, something precious. His mouth found her, Miss Pretty and he worshiped her like he had a point to prove. My body arched, breath hitching with every kiss, every stroke of his tongue.

By the time he entered me, I was already gone.

He slid in deep, so deep it felt like he was stitching me back together from the inside. He filled every inch, slow and controlled, his eyes never leaving mine.

"You feel so damn good," he groaned, gripping my thighs. "I missed you. All of you"

I wrapped around him, hips rising to meet every thrust, every promise.

"I'm right here, Malik," I gasped, my voice breaking. "I'm not going anywhere."

Our bodies moved like they knew the rhythm by heart. It wasn't just sex, and it was soul syncing, that kind of passion that left your body trembling and your heart wide open.

He held me afterward, both of us breathless and soaked in sweat and emotion.

If I could have stopped time, I would have.

But morning came, like it always does.

And I got on that flight body aching, soul full, and heart still tethered to a room at the Marriott in Orlando.

13

REUNITED AND IT FEELS SO DAMN GOOD

Once I got back to Houston, baby, your girl was floating. I couldn't believe it. Malik and I, reunited after twelve years, and it was like we had never skipped a beat. Still goofy. Still effortless. Still us. It was giving soulmate energy, for real.

At first, it started with sweet early morning calls where we would catch up and laugh like old times. But then, one morning, Malik asked for a video chat while he was working. That changed the game. I was at the salon, he was out there being the appliance whisperer, fixing dryers and dishwashers like a boss. We were in two different states, but it felt like we were in the same room, vibing, grinding, living.

What's wild is how the conversations flowed. I guess twelve years of reconnecting will do that. And no, it wasn't like we went radio silent during those years. We would hit each other up for birthdays or send a "Hey stranger" text here and there. But it was nothing like this. Now? Whew. We were all in.

Mornings turned into video chats. As soon as he left the house and I texted, "Top of the day, sexy," that video call would come in. And we would be on the phone damn near all day talking, watching each other work, cracking jokes, falling deeper and deeper.

Back in Ft. Lauderdale, we loved each other, but this was different. Now we were asking real questions. We pulled out the conversation cards, went deep, and got transparent. Back then, our younger selves were more focused on, well, opportunities to get in each other's drawers (let's be honest, lol). But this? The distance made the bond stronger.

We got to know each other.

And then came the monthly visits. Yep. Monthly. It didn't matter who was footing the bill;

I was in Orlando like clockwork. Phone calls and Face Times just weren't enough.

Let's talk about Beach Day.

Now, living in Houston, I do not consider Galveston a real beach, okay? So on one of my visits, I asked, "Babe, can you take me to the beach?" One thing about Malik he might overthink it, but he will get it done.

Clear water, here we come.

Of course, we had to make a few pit stops: Walmart for towels, trunks, and snacks. Then we hit this fire vegetarian spot that had the best sandwiches I've ever had in my life.

And once we got to that beach? We just enjoyed each other. Simple. Beautiful. Real. Malik was different out there, free, relaxed. Maybe because we were far from home, he could let his guard down.

And baby, let me tell you about these big-ass pelicans on the beach looking like they walked off the set of Jurassic Park. Malik had me tucked under his arm like, "If one of them swoops down, I'm throwing this sandwich and running." I said, "Boy, you better not leave me!" He said, "I'm not... but I am throwing the sandwich. Survival first."

At one point, Malik and I waded into the water and just floated there for a while, talking about everything and nothing. The sun on our skin, waves brushing against us—it felt like time had slowed down just for us.

I had one leg wrapped around his waist as we drifted, laughing about the big-ass pelicans flying low like they ran the beach.

"Boy, look at them things," I said. "They act like they own this water."

He laughed, "They probably do. Look at 'em—bold as hell."

I smiled, squinting toward the horizon. "I could really see myself living somewhere like this... waking up to the sound of waves, the air smelling like peace."

Malik tilted his head, studying me for a moment. "Yeah," he said quietly. "It fits you."

I didn't know it then, but I was speaking something into existence—peace, freedom, a life that would one day be mine alone.

When we finally made our way out, my tan swimsuit had started riding up, clinging in all the wrong places. Malik caught a glimpse and grinned, that same slow, knowing look that always made me roll my eyes and smile at the same time.

After a few more "adjustments" and Malik's constant staring, we figured it was time to pack it up before somebody pulled out their phone and turned our little beach date into an Only Fans preview..

THE NIGHTCAP

Malik drove us back with that one-hand-on-the-wheel, one-hand-on-my-thigh energy. Music low, windows down, breeze hitting just right. The sun was setting, and so was the day. But the night? The night was ours.

Back at the Marriott, it was our usual routine. That unspoken vibe. No pressure, no performance. Just us. Laughing, unwinding, still salty from the beach and smelling like coconut and sunshine. He pulled me in like he always does, close, warm, like his arms were the only place that ever made sense.

"You're sandy," he murmured, nuzzling my neck. "The beach did a number on you."

I smiled. "You too. We're both overdue for a rinse."

He kissed my shoulder. "Shower with me."

He didn't have to ask twice.

The steam filled the bathroom, curling around us like a warm whisper. Water streamed down his back, tracing every muscle. I stepped in behind him, hands gliding up his chest, and he let out a low hum, leaning into my touch like it was his lifeline.

His hands found my waist, then my hips, pulling me flush against him. Skin on skin. Heat meeting heat. The water ran over us, but nothing could cool the way we burned for each other.

He turned, his lips capturing mine, hungry, slow, like we had all the time in the world. My back pressed against the slick tile as his mouth moved to my collarbone, tasting the salt left behind by the ocean and the tension building between us.

Soap and water became an afterthought. Our hands weren't washing anymore; we were exploring, rediscovering, reclaiming.

"I need you," he murmured against my neck.

"I'm right here," I breathed.

But the shower, as steamy as it was, couldn't hold what we were about to do.

We stepped out, barely getting wrapped in towels before he scooped me into his arms, carrying me back to the bed like he couldn't wait another second. The moment we hit the sheets, there were no words. Just bodies, breath, the soft thud of hearts racing in sync.

We didn't rush. We didn't pretend. We just felt.

And in that moment, nothing else mattered.

Just the rhythm of us raw, real, and unforgettable.

Who needs Unisom when you have Malik?

THE MORNING AFTER...

I was still in Orlando the next day, my flight wasn't until later, and you already know Malik wasn't letting me leave without spending every minute he could with me.

I was still wrapped in sheets, half-asleep, body hurting so good, when I heard the door open. He had a hotel key (of course, he did), and next thing I knew, he was walking in like he owned the place, Starbucks in hand, looking like a full-blown husband on a mission.

"Wakey wakey," he said, setting the drinks on the nightstand. "I brought us our usual."

And baby, he really meant it.

Our chai teas with oat milk, one extra shot, extra hot at 190 degrees. Don't play with him!

He had the order down to a science.

I sat up with that "I'm trying to be cute, but I just woke up" face, and he handed me my cup like it was a love letter. We sipped, lounged in bed, and just caught up on the random stuff in life, family, work, those "remember when" stories that always made us laugh.

It wasn't even about doing anything big. It was the vibe. The ease. The comfort. We could be in a five-star suite or a folding chair in a parking lot. It would still feel like home if we were next to each other.

Before I had to leave for the airport, Malik ran back out and grabbed us lunch. He came back with those black to-go containers and that proud "I got your favorite" look on his face, like he had just saved the day.

There's a quiet strength in a man who moves with certainty. Running my own world, I'm always in motion, deciding, building, leading. But with Malik, I exhale.

He doesn't ask for control; he simply takes it. With one look, one touch, I forget the weight I carry. He takes the wheel, and I willingly become still. No need for directions. No need for words. Just trust. And a softness I didn't know I missed until he brought it back.

We ate, laughed some more, and even though we both knew the goodbye was creeping up, it didn't feel heavy. It felt like a pause. Not an ending.

When it was finally time to go, he carried my bags, opened the car door, and kissed my forehead like he meant it. And the whole ride to the airport? We were just holding hands, silent sometimes, smiling the whole time.

Because we knew.

This was just one visit. But the way we were moving, there were plenty more to come.

14

REALITY CHECK

It was my off day, and I was deep into doing absolutely nothing when my phone buzzed.

"Top of the day, Sexy Lady."

Just like that, my heart smiled.

I already knew my Sunshine was coming in hot with our usual a.m. text. Then he hit me with:

"Guess where I'm at?"

Huh?! My whole body perked up like I'd just heard Janet Jackson was downstairs.

"Where?"

"You wanna pick me up from the airport?"

BABY! Why did your girl damn near slip in the shower trying to rush to brush my teeth and throw on clothes at the same time? I flew out that door like a woman on a mission.

When I saw him, I froze. My heart couldn't believe it.

"Omg, Malik... you're really here."

"Yeah," he smiled. "I figured I'd change things up. Spend the day with my baby. I fly back tonight. You happy?"

"Hell yeah!" I was cheesing like a fool. I couldn't stop looking at him. I kept glancing over, like, is this real life?

But of course, reality doesn't like to stay quiet too long.

While driving back to my house, my phone pinged a camera notification. Somebody just walked into my house. But hold up... Dante and Tiana were with their fathers this week. Ain't nobody supposed to be there.

Then I hear coughing through the feed. Dante?!

I called him. "What's up? Thought you were staying with your fathers?"

"Yeah, I'm not feeling well," he said. "Too many kids over there, so he brought me back."

I was heated. Not even a call? A heads-up? Nothing? My mood shifted quick.

Malik peeped it. "You good?"

"Dante's home."

"Babe, don't worry. It's cool. Let's just head to the Marriott."

He was so calm, so unbothered. And oh, how I loved that about him.

As soon as we opened the room door, there wasn't a word exchanged. He picked me up like I weighed nothing and laid me on the bed like he was placing fine china. But just as we started getting lost in each other, his phone buzzed.

He ignored it, deep in Ms. Pretty.

It buzzed again. This time, he got up and said, "Let me just put it on silent."

But when he came back, something was off.

His energy? Shifted.

He tried to play it cool, hopping back in like I wouldn't notice. But I noticed. When the Rock of Gibraltar turned into a semi-gummy worm, I sat up.

"Talk to me. What's going on?"

He sighed.

"That was her. She texted me, " I love you.""

We just laid there, holding each other, breathing, thinking.

Turns out, he and Lena had started marriage counseling. Lately, she'd been "coming around." And today? Yeah, this was one of those days.

He looked me in the eyes. I knew he could feel me drifting, knew the shift in me was just as loud as his own.

Then he kissed me soft, deep, with that mix of hunger and guilt.

My rock returned, sliding back into his soft place like he was reclaiming me. But inside, I had drifted. I couldn't help but wonder if this was him proving something to me or to himself. Like he needed me to believe he was still mine.

But I know better.

We made the best of the little time we had left. And then came the drive back to the airport.

Silent.

Just a kiss. And off he went.

Back to reality.

And so did I.

That day marked the beginning of the end of our bubble. Our beautiful, reckless little fantasy world.

As the night settled in, I sat on the edge of my bed, staring at the wall like it had answers. Malik was gone. Dante was resting, and the house had gone still. But my mind, my mind was loud.

For a few hours today, I got to feel like the main character in my own love story. I got swept up, kissed on, and smiled at. He was here with me. And everything felt right until it didn't.

Reality always creeps in.

Because no matter how perfect the day feels, it always ends with him going back to her, back to the life I'm not a part of. I'm not the woman he comes home to; I'm just the woman he escapes with. And that shit is starting to sit heavy on me.

I try to act like it doesn't bother me, like I'm built for this kind of arrangement. But the truth is, I'm not. I want more. I deserve more. And it's getting harder and harder to pretend I don't feel the sting when he leaves.

I used to think loving him was enough, but now I'm starting to wonder if it's actually breaking me.

Down the rabbit hole we continue.

I try to tell myself I need to pull back, that I need to walk away. But then I turn around and send a message like this:

"I'm not ready. You're the first man to have my heart truly. How do I walk away from that? The first time I did, it left me in such a dark place. I'm not ready to wake up and take the red pill yet. I'm choosing to stay in the Matrix until you tell me it's time. You, sir, are a rare one. You are the blueprint.

And then, like clockwork, I wake up to a message like this:

"It's probably not a good time, but I still gotta tell you what I need to say. Your message today was a reflection of exactly how I feel about you, too.

You were sent into my life for a reason, and the more time we spend, the clearer it becomes. It's not something I can explain. It's a feeling that something only you can make me feel. You're the only person I've ever experienced this with.

It's not complicated, I know exactly what it is. You came and changed me. I was in a dark place twice, and both times, you weren't there. But then you came back, right when I needed you most. Maybe it was my spirit calling for you. Maybe it was the universe pulling you back to me. Whatever it was, it felt right. It still does.

That's why I can't help myself when it comes to you. Maybe to the outside world, it doesn't make sense. Maybe it looks wrong. But to me? It's everything. I love you. I need you. I don't know how long this will last until you get tired of me or I mess up again, but right now? I need us.

And I'm not trying to use you. I'm just trying to hold on to something that feels real.

You make me want to move differently. To be better. To go harder. Just to see you smile harder. Shine brighter.

When I'm with you, I feel like I can be me. No fronts. No masks. Just real. You're gorgeous. Your energy? Electric. You're intelligent, vibrant, and powerful. I love you, not like some random, lazy "love." These are facts about you, babe. And I just love you. It is what it is.

If we kept going the way we were... whew, we probably would've made too many babies.

You're sexy as hell, you know that?

I love you. Those are just facts.

And just like that, I'm back. Hooked on every word.

Still chasing the feeling.
Still choosing the Matrix.
Still falling.

15

Reflection 14.5 — The Visit That Shifted Everything

When Malik decided to come visit me in Houston, listen... I was ecstatic. Nobody could've stolen my joy that day. Seeing him sitting next to me in the car? I was straight googly-eyed, gaga, grinning like a teenager. I couldn't believe my baby was actually here. And the wild part? I didn't care if it was for a whole day, an hour, or thirty minutes. The simple fact that he got on a flight just to see me meant everything.

Even though we had a little hiccup with Dante being home sick, none of that mattered. We grabbed our things and headed straight for the Marriott like nothing in the world could shift the joy I had in my chest. It wasn't me going to see him in Orlando this time — he came to me. That meant something. That meant a lot.

We enjoyed ourselves... until we didn't.

Like I mentioned in the chapter, they had started counseling. And Lena would have her "soft days," the days she wanted to reach out and be loving. She chose that exact day — the day he flew to see me — to send one of those messages.

Right in the middle of us being deep into one another, her text came through. He answered, stepped out for a minute, and when he came back... everything shifted. His whole energy changed. And because of how connected we are, I felt it immediately in my body. He explained the situation — the counseling, the shift, her trying, her efforts — and just like that, the mood was gone.

Everyone isn't able to separate emotions the way I can.
   Even a therapist once told me, "You disconnect like a man does."

Maybe it's because I grew up around strong male figures. Maybe it's just how I'm wired. I don't know. I won't pretend I do. But that day did something to me. Something I haven't fully shaken.

Because here's the truth: I would choose Malik every day. Not out of desperation. Not out of fantasy. But because of how he makes me feel when we're together.

I run my own businesses. I'm always making decisions, always in motion, always having to stand firm. I'm a woman every day — but I don't always get to be soft. Softness requires safety. It requires trust. It requires letting someone else take the lead for a moment.

And with Malik?
   It's instant.

It's like somebody hits a switch in my back, and suddenly I'm allowed to be soft, feminine, gentle. I don't have to do everything. I don't have to hold everything. When I'm with him, I get to put down the weight and just... be.

I miss that version of me. The version that feels safe enough to exhale.

But I don't understand how he doesn't see what we have. How he doesn't recognize the difference. Yes, he chose her years ago — but they're not the

70

same people now. And neither are we.

I know he's not fulfilled. I know he feels the shift. I know he feels the love, because I don't love lightly.

But I also know something else.
  Something I've fought against.
  Something I've finally accepted:

As much as I love him, we will not be together in this lifetime.
  That isn't our story.

Because as much as it breaks my heart, he will never make the conscious decision to choose me. Not fully. Not out loud. Not in the way that counts. And if he ever did? It would only be because she left — not because he stood up and claimed me for himself.

And I refuse to be anybody's consolation prize.
  Not now. Not ever.

The man I'm meant for — the man aligned with my next chapter — will choose me first, openly, proudly, and without hesitation. And I'll choose him too.

Until then, I honor the truth:
  Malik holds a place in my story...
  but he is not my ending.

— Liz

16

SISSY-POO KNOWS BEST

I'm a firm believer that everything, every damn thing, happens for a reason. People enter your life as either a lesson or a blessing. Sometimes they're both. And sometimes, they're Malik.

When Malik and I reconnected after (those) twelve years, I knew deep down, in every fiber of my being, that it was finally our time. Everything in me screamed: this is it. All the missed chances, all the detours, all led us back here.

But as fate would have it, he really didn't feel the same.

I needed to get this out of me. I needed to vent.

The only other person I can honestly talk to without feeling judged is my sissy-poo, Rhea. She's just a year younger than me, but somehow she's always been the older one. The wiser one. The one who could read between my silences and pull me back from the ledge with just a look or a laugh. It's always refreshing knowing I have her to go to when my thoughts start getting too loud, too tangled.

So naturally, when my heart started spiraling again, I picked up the phone and reached out.

"Girl, I'm tripping," I told her. "Like, for real. I thought I had control over this, but I'm back under. And I know better, but I still can't help myself."

Rhea didn't hit me with a lecture. She didn't say, "I told you so."
   She just listened.
   She always listens.

Sometimes, that's all I need.
   Other times? I need her to remind me who the hell I am.
   And when it comes to Malik, I lose that sometimes. I lose myself.

But Rhea?
   She finds me every time.

Just a heads-up about Rhea; that girl's got a gift.
   She's like a human lie detector mixed with a therapist and just a sprinkle of voodoo. You show her a picture, and she'll tell you exactly what that person's going through. Sad?
   Hiding something? Frontin'? She sees it all. It's like her eyes were designed to read souls instead of selfies.

So I sent her a pic of Malik and asked, "What do you see?"

Rhea: I see some sadness... smiling through sadness.
   Nia: Yeah... It's a sad situation.
   Rhea: Well, y'all can unsadden it
   Nia: Lol... I'm going the other route, though.
   Rhea: Sad.
   Rhea: I like to root for true love.
   Nia: I'm so sad
   Rhea: I'm sorry, sis.

Nia: Yeah... Like, I just don't understand. He says we're soulmates. That we're connected mentally, physically, spiritually and yet he still doesn't want to see where this can go. Still dealing with the same issues with his wife that he had when we first met. Like, WTF?!

I'm sitting here thinking we reconnected so we could finally be together.
But to him? It was just to "pull him out of a funk."

How selfish is that?

Arrrrrrgh!

Omg. You wouldn't even believe the dream I once had...
Bottom line?
Malik thinks I'll always be here. Waiting.

The fuck not.

I'm nobody's consolation prize.
I'm the fucking GRAND PRIZE.

Nia: Sorry. I just needed to vent.
Rhea: Wow... yeah, that is selfish. He needs a hard ultimatum. You can't be good enough to be his everything but not good enough to be his wife. Everything he said in that voicemail, talking about "You're mine." Nah. No, nigga your wife is yours.

Nia: Yeah... this hurts.
Rhea: Yeah... this hurts. But you gotta remember something, this ain't about your worth. It's about his limitations. You're not asking for too much; you're just asking the wrong one to give it.

Nia: Whew... say that again.

Rhea: Sis, don't shrink to fit into the cracks of somebody else's confusion. You were made for light. You were made for more. He's comfortable in chaos. But you? You're not built to sit in someone's "maybe."

You're the grand prize, remember?
  Act accordingly.

And with that... she found me.

Again.

17

WHEN THE KIDS KNOW

So, even though I started spiraling again, slipping down that familiar rabbit hole of sadness, Malik and I still kept up our video chats.

I was still smiling. Still laughing. Still pretending everything was fine.

But the ones who know me best? They weren't fooled.

One night, I got off the phone with Malik, and as I closed my laptop, I turned to see Dante and Tiana watching me with those eyes. Those knowing, loving, concerned eyes.

"Mom," Dante started, his voice low but steady, "you good?"

I opened my mouth to say I'm fine, but for once... I didn't have the energy to lie.

So I told them.

Told them that their mom, the one who preaches self-worth and strength, was entangled in something messy. That I was in love with a man who was married. That he'd been in my life a long time, and it wasn't simple. That I knew it wasn't very easy and probably didn't make sense to them... but that he meant something to me.

And that's when the floodgates opened.

Tiana, my sweet girl, sat quietly, her eyes glossy with emotion. But Dante? Whew. My son? He was pissed.

"You deserve better, Ma," he said, voice tight. "We've seen the video chats.

We hear you laughing. But your eyes... they don't smile like your mouth does."

He sat on the edge of my bed, shaking his head like he was trying to make sense of something that didn't add up.

"And Malik? He's a hypocrite. How can you say you love someone so much, but stay with somebody else just because you have kids together? That doesn't make sense.

That's not love. That's fear."

His words hit me like bricks.

I didn't expect my children to be the ones telling me what I should've already known. But there they were, my truth-tellers. And honestly? I needed to hear it.

Tiana finally spoke, "I just want you to be happy, Mommy. And I don't think he makes you happy all the time... just sometimes. And sometimes it isn't enough for someone like you."

Whew.

I sat there in silence, letting their words wash over me like a baptism I didn't ask for but clearly needed.

They were right.

I was deserving of more. Of better. Of whole love not borrowed, not rationed.

The next morning hit different. Not because it was brighter or quieter, but because everything that was said the night before still echoed in my chest like it was on a loop.

I lay in bed a little longer than usual, not scrolling, not checking emails, just... still.

Letting their words marinate.

Dante's voice was the loudest in my head.

"You deserve better, Ma."

It wasn't even what he said; it was how he said it, like a man. Like he wasn't just my son anymore, but someone who saw me, really saw me and didn't like what I'd become.

And Tiana? She just held my hand as I cried in silence after they both left the room. My baby girl didn't say anything else. She didn't have to. She'd said enough.

It's a different kind of heartbreak when your children show you your reflection. No filters. No soft landings. Just the truth. Raw. Undeniable. And somehow, still filled with love.

But even with all that... I still picked up my phone.

Still sent him a "Good morning" text like nothing had changed.

"Top of the day, babe."

And the thing is, I didn't even want a response. I just needed him to know I was still there. That despite the tears, the heartbreak, the disappointment from my own children,

I hadn't let go. Not yet.

The phone buzzed.

"Hey, baby. You good?"

I paused.

And for the first time in a long time, I didn't answer right away.

Because no, I wasn't good.

I felt exposed, stripped of all the lies I'd been telling myself. And the worst part? It wasn't Malik, who broke me open, it was my babies, my own flesh and blood. And they weren't wrong.

I sat on the edge of the bed, the weight of it all pulling my shoulders down. My room felt smaller somehow, like the walls were inching closer, forcing me to choose: stay buried in this cycle or fight for a way out.

But love, especially the kind that's tangled in years of memories, what-ifs, and stolen moments, isn't something you just walk away from after one hard conversation. So I breathed. Deeply. Slowly. And whispered to myself, "You're going to be okay. Just not all at once."

Later that day, Malik called like he always did, video chat, the usual smile, that familiar. "What's up, beautiful?" But this time, I couldn't fake it. Malik could sense something was off. Even through the screen, he could feel it my energy had shifted.

"Nia... what's wrong?" he asked gently, concern lining his voice. I took a breath, eyes glistening with the weight of the conversation I had with my children the night before. "I talked to Dante and Tiana," I said, my voice barely above a whisper. "They've seen us on video calls. They know what's going on. And they reminded me of something I've been ignoring for too long." He didn't interrupt. He just listened.

"I've been choosing you, Malik. Over my peace, over my growth, even over my children's unspoken judgment. But last night, they made it clear Mama deserves better. And you know what? They're right." My voice trembled but didn't break.

"I love you," I said, letting the words sit heavy in the air between us. "But I can't keep being the one waiting in the wings while you try to make something work with someone else. You need to focus on your marriage. And I..." I paused, eyes lowered. "I need to focus on me."

He closed his eyes, pain flickering across his face. "So what are you saying?"

"I'm saying we have to end this. Not because I don't love you, but because I finally love me more."

The silence that followed was the kind that said everything. Neither of us hung up. We just sat there, eyes locked through the screen, the connection fading not from signal loss but from the slow, inevitable goodbye that needed no words.

As the screen finally dimmed and the call ended, not by a press of a button but by the weight of silence, I just sat there, staring at my reflection. My heart felt heavy, but for the first time in a long time, it didn't feel confused.

I wasn't waiting for a reply. I wasn't hoping he'd say he'd leave. I wasn't spiraling. I was still.

Still, and finally at peace with my decision.

Choosing myself didn't mean I stopped loving him. It meant I finally started loving myself more. And maybe that's what hurt the most, that I should have done this a long time ago.

But now? I'm done being the woman who waits.

I'm done being the woman who pretends she's okay with being "almost."
I'm done choosing love that doesn't choose me back completely.

I wiped a single tear, stood up from the bed, and whispered to myself:

This time, I choose myself.

"Sometimes the hardest part of letting go isn't the goodbye; it's realizing you were never holding onto love, just the hope that it would become it."

18

ECHOS IN THE SILENCE

So, after finally choosing myself, I thought I'd feel free. Whole. Healed.

Instead, I threw myself into everything but healing. Work. The kids. Business plans. Distractions dressed up as progress.

I even downloaded a dating app, swiped through maybe four or five profiles, then deleted it the next morning. Because the truth is, I wasn't ready. Not to flirt. Not to share my space. Not to pretend I was okay when I was still unraveling inside.

I was still crying in the shower. Still pouring more drinks than I poured love into myself. Still staring at my phone like maybe... just maybe he'd reach out.

I told Dante and Tiana I needed a little space. They didn't take it personally; they knew I was in one of my moods. But this wasn't just a mood. This was grief.

Grieving a man who was still very much alive, but suddenly unreachable.

When I say Malik blocked me, I mean blocked me. Whats App. Gone. Instagram. Vanished. Facebook? Nope. Even my number couldn't get through.

I'd send messages only to watch them sit there unsent, undelivered like my love, waiting in limbo.

That silence? It wasn't peaceful. It wasn't kind.

Two weeks passed. Two long, aching, soul-checking weeks.

Then I did something bold. Desperate, maybe... but bold.

I used my work phone.

Typed this message. Held my breath. And hit send.

You just took the crown. Imagine someone telling you they're in love with you...But they can't be with you because they're married.

Imagine hearing them say they were never in love with the person they married... But they're staying because they made a promise to God.

Imagine that same person looking you in the eye and saying,"If I were you, I would've let go."

Now, tell me how would you feel?

I'm 46 years young, and I've only ever truly been in love with one man. You.

Imagine keeping your distance from someone for over a decade...Only to reconnect 12 years later, and it feels like no time has passed. Like the universe just unpaused a love story that had been waiting for the right moment. Like, this was finally our time.

But then, just like that, you're hit with the truth:

The love of your life says he loves you... But he can't choose you.

Because he wants to respect the vows he made. Yet he still flies you in. Still sees you monthly. Still Face Times you six days out of the week.

I always say I'm the biggest hypocrite I know...But congratulations, babe you won this round.

Malik's Response:

I didn't block you out of hate. I blocked you because I didn't know what else to do. Everything about this... us... was starting to tear me apart, and I didn't know how to keep pretending like I had it under control. I told myself I needed space, silence, distance, whatever I had to do to protect what little peace I had left. But the truth is, none of it worked. You still live in my mind, every damn day. When I saw your name pop up from that work number, my heart dropped. Part of me wanted to ignore it. Pretend like I didn't feel anything anymore. But the other part, the real part, just missed you. Missed your voice. Missed you being mine, even if you never really could be.

I read your message over and over. Yeah, it stung. But it was honest. Too honest.

And maybe I deserved every word of it.

You called me a hypocrite. Maybe I am. Because I tell you I love you, but I don't choose you. I say I want you happy, but I keep showing up in ways that only make it harder. I talk about honoring vows, but my heart's been with you for years.

And you're right, I probably did win the crown. But it never felt like winning. It felt like losing you, piece by piece.

I wish I had better answers. I wish I could rewrite time. But all I can say right now is... I still love you. Deep. Ugly. All-consuming love.

And I don't know what to do with it.

So I just carry it. Every day.

Nia's Reply:

Please unblock me.

That's all I ask.

I didn't send a paragraph. No follow-up. Just those four words, sitting there, heavy but tender like a hand held out in the dark.

And he felt it.

A minute passed. Then two.

Then the phone lit up. Face Time: Malik.

My breath caught in my throat as I answered. There he was. No words. Just that half-smile he always gave me when he didn't know what to say but felt everything.

And there I was, eyes soft, face flushed from holding back tears I didn't want him to see.

For a few seconds, we just looked at each other. Foolish. Familiar. Home. Neither one spoke. We didn't have to. That look said it all.

Here we go again. Back down the rabbit hole. Together.

19

CLOUD 9....AGAIN

So, yep. Here we were again, Malik and I, jumping off that emotional cliff hand in hand like we had parachutes made of hope with just a sprinkle of delusion. It's wild how we could have a blow-up one day, and the next... It's like it never happened. No grudges. No awkward silences. Just right back to laughing, flirting, finishing each other's sentences.

If we were in a real relationship, that would be kind of amazing. But we weren't, so instead, it felt more like emotional whiplash dressed up as romance.

Meanwhile, back in my real life, I was out here thriving. The salon was lit, locs getting loved on, braids braided to perfection, and the vibes? Immaculate. I was in my zone, doing what I do best: making people feel good from the roots, literally.

But hair wasn't my only passion. My other love? Food. Feeding folks and watching their eyes close on that first bite like they just saw heaven? Whew, baby. So instead of bouncing from one pop-up shop to the next, I started looking for a space where I could bring both my worlds together. Natural hair and home-cooked flavor under one roof? Yeah, the dream was finally starting to look like reality.

And Malik? He was leveling up, too. Leaving the residential appliance game behind and stepping into the big leagues: commercial appliance repair. He was hyped, said he was tired of fixing the same boring dishwashers and stoves. This new opportunity came with months of training... in Jersey.

You already know what that meant.

Flights were booked. Edges laid. Luggage packed with more lingerie than outerwear.

Because when my man, ahem, the man I was deeply entangled with called, I answered. Jersey became our little love bubble. Hotels. Room service. Face Time. Good mornings that turned into "open the door" surprises.

But even before I packed a bag, our conversations had already taken us there.

"Top of the day, Gorgeous You better have an amazing day 'cause you're already in it. Love you Beautiful ," he texted.

I couldn't help but smile. "Top of the day, My GoGetter 🍫," I shot back.

"I love you too, babe ." "I miss you more, Babe ."

That back-and-forth? Ugh. It had me floating.

He told me not to worry about a rental. "I'll send a car to pick you up when you land," he said, like a true gentleman.

I was like, "Ok 💋," but in my head? I was screaming, YES LAWD!

I remember texting him, "Do you stay straight for the 3 weeks or go home on the weekends?" He replied, "First weekend I go home, but the second one I stay."

"Wheels are turning lol," I messaged. He hit me with a "smh 🤦🏿‍♂️." And I said, "Yours wasn't?"

(We both knew where this was going.)

That's when I asked if he'd be in Jersey on the 25th and 26th, trying to plan my little sneak-away. He said, "Nah, I fly back the 25th, come back the 28th and stay till November 8th."

Boom. We had a window.

October 18th rolled around, and I was feeling' myself. "Who just got freshly waxed... MEEEEEEEEE!!!!" I texted.

He didn't even try to hide the excitement.

"I can taste her already."

"You coming up Monday or Tuesday?" "Tuesday the 22nd." "Okay, I need the flight info. I'll send the car; the key will be at the front desk."

That's when he realized how quick my trip was.

"YOU'RE ONLY STAYING FOR ONE DAY!?" "Then we are NOT sleeping that night." "I get it, you got clients…"

I told him, "Yes ," but I wasn't about to waste one minute. "Nope ."

Even if I couldn't cancel every client, I was gonna make it work.

I asked if he was excited for training.

His response?

"More excited to see you than I am about training. That's facts."

Whew. Say less.

On the 20th, I hit him with, "Top of the day 💋." He responded, "Top of the day, Sexy." Then I sent, "Counting down…" His reply? "I'm right there with you, Babe. I can't wait."

Neither could I.

It's funny how something as small as a text can feel like a full-body hug when it's from the right person. Every morning felt like we were unwrapping little pieces of each other through those messages. And with each passing hour, the countdown got louder in my spirit.

Forget a carry-on, I rolled up with a whole kitchen set. Pots, pans, seasonings, and enough flavor to start a food truck. TSA probably thought I was catering a wedding. But nope, just heading to Jersey to cook for Malik for the first time. I wasn't playing. This man was about to find out I don't just serve looks, I serve plates. Clothes? Eh, I packed a few. But that luggage was 90% culinary ambition and 10% "just in case" lingerie.

The night before my flight, I couldn't sleep. My mind was rehearsing all the moments I imagined we'd have our first kiss when I got there, the way he'd grab my bags and pull me into him like time hadn't passed. The way he'd probably clown me for crying… and then hold me tighter because he'd missed me just the same.

It's crazy how love can make hours feel like days, and days feel like months when you're waiting on a moment.

But this moment? Oh, this moment was about to be ours.

And even though I knew it wouldn't last forever, hell, it was just one day, I was gonna soak up every second like it was a lifetime.

Because sometimes, it ain't about how long it lasts.

It's about how deep it hits.

The moment the car turned into the hotel driveway, I spotted him.

Leaning against the column near the entrance, hands tucked in his pockets like a whole leading man. He wasn't even trying, and still looked like he stepped out of a GQ Magazine. My stomach did a full somersault. I wasn't even fully out of the car yet, and he had me weak.

He walked over before the driver could even put the car in park. Opened the door for me.

Said nothing at first, just looked.

Not just a glance, either. One of those pull-your-soul-out-your-chest stares.

"Hey, baby," he finally said, his voice low and thick, like molasses.

I stepped out, heels striking the pavement, and before I could even think, my hand was on his face. I touched him softly, slowly, as if I had to make sure he was really there and not just some fantasy I'd conjured up mid-flight.

And then he kissed me.

Not a "hi" kiss.

Not a "glad-you're-here" kiss..

It was the kind of kiss that robbed the air from the entire Tri-State area. A kiss that made time irrelevant. One of those, don't talk, just feel this kind of kiss.

I felt my luggage drop to the ground. Literally, my bag hit the pavement, and I didn't even flinch.

He pulled back just enough to whisper, "Damn, I missed you."

I exhaled the breath I hadn't even realized I'd been holding for weeks.

Then, like the gentleman he always was when he was mine, he picked up my bags, slid his hand down my back, and led me inside.

And just like that, I was exactly where I wanted to be. With him.

The elevator ride was silent, but it wasn't quiet. Our bodies were doing all the talking.

His hand rested on the small of my back, warm, intentional. My heart? Beating like I owed it rent. I caught him peeking at me in the reflection of the elevator doors, and I bit my bottom lip just to keep from smirking too hard.

"What?" I finally asked, eyes still forward.

"Nothing," he said, his voice already laced with trouble. "You know exactly what."

Ding. Floor seven.

He led me to the room, swiped the key card, and held the door open like the gentleman he was. I walked in, trying to act unfazed like I wasn't already melting.

The room smelled of cologne and fresh linens. Lights low. Mood high.

"You packed light," he teased, eyeing my over sized suitcase.

"First of all," I shot back, "don't judge me. A queen needs options."

"A queen?" He smirked, stepping closer. "That right there? That's what I missed. That mouth."

"Oh, you missed this mouth?" I raised a brow.

"Don't play with me, Nia."

And just like that, the tension snapped back like a stretched rubber band. He stood in front of me now, close enough for my perfume to cling to him, but still not touching.

"You really came," he said, eyes searching mine.

"I really did," I replied. "Told you my wheels were turning."

"You always were the wild one," he said, smiling.

"And you always know how to bring her out."

He brushed a curl from my cheek and let his fingers linger just a second too long. My knees whispered a prayer.

"You hungry?" he asked.

"For food or..."

"See?" He laughed, stepping back. "There goes that mouth again."

"You brought it out of retirement. So you deal with it." "Gladly," he said, heading towards the mini-fridge. "But first, let me feed you. I need you over sized."

I shook my head, laughing, finally letting my body drop onto the bed. "You ain't changed."

He glanced over his shoulder and grinned.

"Neither have you. Still fine as hell. Still mine for now."

Whew. My stomach was growling, but not just from hunger.

After we ate well, picked at the food between flirting, eye contact, and inside jokes, it was like the walls of the room started to breathe with us. The energy was humming, thick and low, and neither of us needed to say what came next.

"Come shower with me," I said softly, already pulling my curls into a loose bun.

He didn't hesitate. He just stood up, grabbed two towels, and followed me into the bathroom like he'd been waiting on those four words all day.

The steam rose fast, fogging up the mirror as hot water hit cool tile. I stepped in first, letting the warmth melt away every trace of the outside world. When he stepped in behind me, his hands were gentle but certain, like he remembered every dip and curve of me even after all this time.

He lathered me slowly, as if he were learning me again, fingertips tracing collarbones, shoulders, waist... places that didn't just make me shiver, they made me feel seen.

I turned to face him, the water washing over both of us as our foreheads met, and the silence said everything.

"You good?" he whispered.

"I'm home," I breathed.

After the shower, he dried me off with the kind of care that'll have your soul leaning back. He laid me across the bed, then opened his duffle bag like he was about to fix a sink, except instead of tools, he pulled out a small bottle of warm oil.

"Face down," he said, low and raspy. "Let me love on you."

The first touch had me arching my back like a prayer. His hands started at my shoulders, kneading in slow, deep strokes, easing out stress I hadn't even realized I was holding. The oil was warm. His touch? Warmer.

He worked his way down my spine, across my hips, along my thighs, pausing just enough to make me squirm but not beg. He was focused. Patient. Intentional. Every touch felt like a love letter written in silence.

89

Then I turned over. And that's when it got... deeper.

The way he looked at me like I was fragile but also the most powerful thing in the room made my breath catch.

He started again. Chest. Stomach. Inner thighs. Slow.He didn't rush. He didn't ask.

He just read me, as if the whole of me were poetry and he'd been studying every line in secret.

By the time he reached inside, it wasn't just a massage anymore; it was a connection. We weren't just skin to skin... we were soul to soul. The kind of intimacy that didn't just make you moan, it made you feel safe. Made you remember what being wanted fully felt like.

He moved with purpose. Listened to every breath, every shiver. And when I finally came undone beneath him, it wasn't just release, it was surrender.

And when he held me afterwards, tracing lazy circles on my back, I swear the silence between us was louder than anything we'd ever said.

The Morning After

I woke up to the scent of his warm skin, a hint of cologne, and something that smelled like peace. His arm was still wrapped around me, our legs tangled like neither of us ever wanted to move. I wasn't sure how long we had before he had to leave, but I wasn't ready to let go just yet.

He stirred before I did. Moved slowly, like he didn't want to break the spell.

"You good?" he whispered, voice low and sleepy, brushing a kiss across my shoulder.

I nodded, eyes still closed, pulling the covers up a little higher just to hold on to that last ounce of comfort.

He slid out of bed, moving quietly through the room, grabbing his training gear, laying it out like clockwork. I watched him through cracked lashes, focused, grounded, everything I loved about him wrapped in that morning calm.

There's something about watching a man get dressed that just hits different. The way he pulled on his shirt, slid on his watch, adjusted his collar like he was about to conquer something. He wasn't even trying, and still... whew.I must've sighed without realizing.

"What?" he asked, catching me peeking at him.

"Nothing," I said with a sleepy smirk. "Just admiring the view."

"Oh yeah?" He chuckled, walking back over to the bed. "This view is gonna miss you too."

He leaned down, brushed the curls from my forehead, and placed the softest kiss right between my eyes. Not rushed. Not out of obligation. The kind of kiss that speaks: I see you. I appreciate you. I'll carry this moment with me today.

"I'll be back later," he said, standing up again. "But you go back to sleep. Rest that beautiful body. You earned it."

He winked before grabbing his bag and heading to the door.

And just like that, the room felt a little emptier, but my heart? It felt full.

20

HONEY, I'M HOME

So, like I said before, your girl came prepared, I wasn't just pulling up cute; I pulled up ready to chef it all the way up. I made escovitch fish, rice and peas, and fried some plantain to a perfect golden crisp. I was just waiting on my Walmart delivery like it was an Amazon Prime sponsorship deal. As soon as the last item hit the doorstep, I got busy in that kitchen. And let me tell you, it felt good. Really good.

This was the first time Malik was tasting my food. After all our conversations about how much I love to cook and the pop-up shops I've done, he was finally getting the full experience. I was low-key nervous but mostly excited to see his reaction.

It was around the time he usually came home, and sure enough, the door opened and he called out, "Honey, I'm home!" I was in the kitchen like, "I'm right here, baby!" just cheesin' over the stove like I was in some Black love Netflix movie.

He walked in, and I met him at the door with a hug and a kiss so sweet it could've been dessert. I looked him dead in the eyes and said, "Go get your ass in the shower. I got something for you." He started sniffing the air like a cartoon character and said, "Damn, it smells so good in here."

And in that moment? It really felt like we lived together. Just me, him, and the scent of love and fried plantain.

By the time Malik got out of the shower, steam still trailing behind him like he'd walked straight out of a slow-motion dream, I already had our food plated. His cognac was waiting for him like a loyal sidekick, and my Taylor Port glistened in my glass like it knew what kind of night it was about to be.

He sat down, towel draped around his neck, still glistening from the shower, and gave me this look like he was trying to figure out how I'd gone from girlfriend to private chef overnight.

"You did all this?" he asked, biting into a plantain like it was his first taste of heaven. "Yes, baby. I told you, I don't play in the kitchen." He took another bite, groaning a little. "Damn. I should've married you when I had the chance." I sipped my drink and gave him a teasing smirk. "Well, look who just realized I'm wife material." He winked. "Nah, I've been known. I just thought you came with a warning label: Highly Addictive." I laughed, butterflies fluttering in my chest. "And you still overdosed, huh?" He leaned in a little, fork still in hand. "If this food doesn't kill me, you definitely will."

He cleaned that plate like he was trying to impress a Jamaican aunty. Every last morsel. Then he pushed it aside, looked me dead in the eyes and said, "Now what I really wanna taste... is dessert."

I raised a brow. "Oh? You still got room after all that?" He licked his lips. "For you? Always."

Whew. Baby, I was dessert.

I didn't want to leave the next morning. My body was in motion, but my heart stayed curled up in his bed.

The morning came wrapped in quiet. No alarms. No urgency. Just the soft hum of the city waking up outside the hotel window and the even softer ache of knowing it was time to go.

We moved slow, savoring every second. I got dressed while Malik stood at the sink, brushing his beard, glancing at me in the mirror like he didn't want to blink and miss a moment.

He threw on his work gear, and I pulled my curls into a messy bun. We weren't rushing, just moving through the motions like two people trying to hold on to the night.

As we headed down for breakfast, he nudged me with a smirk. "You sure you can't call out today?"

I looked at him sideways. "Call out? Baby, I am the job."

He laughed, shaking his head. "My bad, Miss Boss Moves."

We sat in the hotel café over chai tea, eggs, and stolen glances. Nothing fancy, but it felt... satisfying. His knee brushed mine under the table, and his eyes kept finding their way back to me, like he was memorizing my face for later.

"You always surprise me," he said, staring at his plate. "The way you move, the way you love... the way you cook."I smiled, sipping my chai tea. "You sound like a man who just got fed and handled.""Exactly that," he said, eyes low, lips curled into a grin. "And now you've got me going to work like everything's normal."

Outside, the Uber Black he'd ordered was already waiting."You didn't have to do that," I said as he grabbed my bag." I know," he replied. "That's why I did it."

He opened the door for me, but neither of us moved just yet. His hand lingered at my waist, his lips pressed to my forehead, and for a second, it felt like goodbye wasn't coming.

"I'm proud of you," he whispered. "For everything." "I'm proud of us," I said, my voice barely above the hum of the city. "No regrets."

He nodded, stepping back as I climbed in. I rolled the window down, and he leaned in one last time.

"Text me when you land," he said.

"I will."

And then the door closed, and I was gone.

But not empty. I left full of memories, of kisses, of warmth. He may not be mine forever...

But he was mine last night.

And that was enough.

21

HOLDING UP THE MIRROR

The goodbye had already begun, but I hadn't landed yet.

My body was still humming from our time together, sore in the best kind of ways, but my heart? Somewhere in between gates, trying to hold on to every last bit of us. Airports are cruel like that. They rush your body forward while your soul stays behind, tangled in the sheets, stuck in the silence after his last kiss.

I was texting him with a smile on my lips and a lump in my throat. The last twenty-four hours played in my mind like a love song with no chorus, just verses that made me melt. No hook. Just him. And me. And the kind of memories you don't get to make twice.

And then it happened.

A Facebook memory popped up. Fourteen years ago. Same date. Same man. Different versions of us.

23 October 2010 "I don't pretend to know what love is for everyone, but for me, love is knowing all about someone, and still wanting to be with them more than any other person. Love is trusting them enough to tell them everything about yourself, including the things you might be ashamed of. Love is feeling comfortable and safe with someone, but still getting weak knees when they walk into a room and smile at you... Love is love. "And just below it:

"Missing my Bae!!!!!"

THE OTHER SIDE OF THE BED

I didn't name him. I never had to. Only he knew.

So I shared it quietly, boldly with a single caption:"14 years ago 💋"

He saw it immediately. Because he always did.

Malik: I'm going to love this post over again.

Nia: I'm guessing this is Our New Chapter... I asked Our Heavenly Father to bless us with Our Happy Ending... whatever that will be 💋

Malik: It's our New Beginning... and it's going to be amazing, filled with sadness, joy, blessings, and love.

Malik:I love every single minute we had together. To know that you can love me the way you do is something I've kept close and protected. "I love you" is not enough to express how I feel or who I am about you. That could never have an end, just a New Chapter for your book.

Tears threatened to spill.

I held them back with a half-smile, half-sob.

Nia: At the airport ◼

Malik: I see you ◼

It felt like he was right there, watching me from the other side of the terminal, whispering "I love you" between glances.

Nia: I, too, enjoyed our time together... it felt like we were in a tiny apartment with lots of love. When you came home from work, my ass was so excited to see you... MY HEART ❤!!!!

Malik: I felt the same way. I was excited to get home and hold you... especially with your nipples looking at me, looking at them.

Nia: You're so silly lol. Have another great day at work, Babe 💋

Nia: On the plane

Reality hit.

No more moments. No more touches. Just sky and distance between us now.

Nia: Home.

Malik: Good, I can breathe now lol. I love you, babe

Nia: I love you 💋...I'm sad, but not if that makes sense.

Malik: Don't be like that.

Nia: Call me later... It's a weird feeling.

That in-between space, the grief before grief, the goodbye before it's final.

I was still in the air, but my heart was already on the ground, with him.

Malik: Okay.

Nia: How's training?

Malik: We're getting into the technical part the fun part. But I've been feeling sad since you left. The room and my heart feel like something is missing.

Nia: The fun part... schematics, lol if I spelled that right. I miss us too!!! Omg, everything is hurting so good 😊

The soreness reminded me it was real. That I had been with him. That it wasn't a dream.

But the ache in my chest reminded me it was over... for now.

We hadn't fully said goodbye. But the landing was coming.

And the next chapter? Still unwritten. Still wide open.

Check your email.

That was the message I woke up to. No "Top of the day," no "Hey gorgeous," just: Check your email.

So I did, still half-asleep, thinking it was something random. But there it was.

A round-trip flight. Jersey. One week.

He really booked the tickets. No warning. No "What do you think?"

Just boom. Round-trip to Jersey. A whole week with him.

That kind of move? Bold. Assertive in a way that made my heart do back flip and my hormones start break dancing.

Because in that moment, all I could think was: My man, my man, my man.

Now, don't get it twisted. He's not my man, not officially. But that feeling? Oh, it was real. That moment when someone chooses you like that, makes space for you like that...Whew. It did something to me.

Had me smiling like a fat kid with a fork and a full slice of cake. Not even birthday cake, just because-you're-happy cake.

And the truth is, it wasn't even about the flight. It was what it meant that he wanted time. Not just a night. Not just a moment.

A whole damn week.

With me.

I landed in Jersey around 2 p.m.

He sent a black car to pick me up like I was somebody's Grammy-nominated girlfriend. I slid into the backseat with my black fur coat wrapped around me like I had a security team waiting at the hotel. It was cold as hell out there, 18 degrees. I don't even understand that kind of disrespectful weather anymore. My bones weren't built for that.

I made a couple of stops, but once I got to the hotel, there he was. My baby. Arms open. Smile wide.

He embraced me like he always does, like he knew I was the missing piece he'd been waiting for. I just let myself melt into him.

My heart was full. Just knowing we were about to have a whole week together made my soul stretch out like it had room to breathe again.

He planned a date night, too. Told me to bring something sexy. And baby, I understood the assignment. Red dress. Heels. Hair laid.

Walking beside him into that beautiful restaurant, I felt like the leading lady in a movie that didn't end in heartbreak.

He looked at me like I was art. We ate. We laughed. He held my hand across the table. But... something was off. I felt it.

Not loud. Not obvious. But present. Like a draft sneaking through a cracked window.

We didn't talk about it that night, though. I just tucked the feeling away.

The rest of the week was sweet for the most part. But then the calls started. Her calls.

She would call, and he wouldn't step outside. He'd answer it on speaker... like I needed to hear that part of his life.

And maybe he thought it would make things feel honest or less like a secret. But hearing them laugh? Hearing her giggle in that I-know-you kind of way? That cut deep.

I sat there, listening to his wife sound like the woman I wanted to be.

And even though I knew I was the other woman...

I was still a woman.

With feelings. With dreams. With hope that maybe just maybe I'd be chosen one day.

But I swallowed it. Faked the funk like I'd done so many times before.

We went grocery shopping like a little married couple, picking out vegetables for the vegan soup I was about to put my foot in. And when I say I did that, I mean he slurped that bowl like it was his last meal. Devoured it.

We played games, what's it called? Twister? Yeah, the one with the colored circles. And of course, he said I cheated. He said tall people shouldn't be allowed to play anyway. We laughed.

We curled up watching movies. He didn't even trade that week. That blew me away because that man loves his trading. But I guess, for those few days, he loved our time more.

And I did too.

But when I got back to Texas…Something shifted.

That trip was beautiful, but it left me heavy. The highs were so high, but the lows were gut-deep. And when your heart has to keep flipping itself inside out to survive, you start to wonder what kind of damage you're doing just to feel good for a moment.

So I made the call.

To a therapist.

Because loving him was starting to cost me peace.

And I deserve more than a week of pretending.

I deserve a forever that doesn't come with mute buttons and guilt.

I started seeing this new therapist, and honestly? I was really enjoying the sessions.

She listens like, really listens. Not just the nod-and-smile kind, but the kind that makes you feel seen without feeling judged.

She doesn't hand out advice like fortune cookies either. No, she makes you think.

Makes you sit in the middle of your mess and ask yourself: How did I get here?

But whew, this one question?

This one question stopped me in my tracks.

"Why are you exhibiting low-vibrational actions when you are not a low-vibrational woman?"

Let me tell you that one hit different.

I sat there, stuck.

Because what do you say when someone mirrors your truth back to you?

And after sitting with it, really sitting with it, I had to face something I never wanted to admit out loud:

I loved Malik more than I loved myself.

And baby... that's low-vibrational as hell.

That's the kind of love that drains you.

That has you betraying your boundaries, your worth, your peace...

All in the name of trying to hold on to someone who never had the capacity to hold you.

It made me realize that being high-vibe isn't about crystals and quotes and pretending everything's okay.

It's about choosing yourself consistently.

It's about not dimming your light for someone who won't even meet you halfway in the dark.

So now, I'm sitting with the truth and asking myself:

What would it look like to love me like I love him?

Because that is the vibration I deserve to be on.

22

Chapter X - THE MOVADO

We didn't argue like other couples. No shouting. No cursing. Just conversations that carried weight, where one word could cut deeper than a scream. This one started with a watch.

Nia's Voice:

Malik had been grinding hard, running his own appliance business, making real moves.

I was proud of him. So proud, I wanted to mark the moment. A Movado watch is sharp, sleek, and professional.

Something that said: I see you. I honor you.

But the surprise unraveled the second Movado called me to confirm a signature. I had to tell him. And once he knew, he started searching for Movado watches on his computer like he was gifting himself.

Then came the kicker, his wife glanced at the screen and said:

Her: "Oh, so we're getting Movado watches now?"

The next day, he told me about it.

Nia: "And what did you say?"

Malik: "I told her I'll think about it."

The nerve. My stomach twisted.

Nia: "You'll think about it? Malik, she's not working. She's at home. You're busting your ass, building everything with your own hands, and she wants a watch too? Why? That gift was for you. For your grind. Why can't you just accept that without dragging her into it?"

But what I really wanted to say was: I already know you're going to buy her one. And it feels like I just opened the door for her gift, while mine gets erased.

Nia: "So let me guess... you're actually gonna buy her one, right?"

Malik: "She's my wife, Nia. If I want to buy her a watch, I can. That doesn't erase what you did."

But it did. Because he hadn't once said thank you. Not once acknowledged the thought I put into him. My green-eyed monster clawed to the surface.

Nia: "You didn't even thank me. Not once. Do you know how that makes me feel? Like you have to camouflage your blessing just to keep the peace at home. And meanwhile, I'm left looking like... nothing."

I let it all out in a text rant that night, saying flat out he looked like he couldn't stand on his own two feet. Like his wife ran the show.

— -

Malik's Voice:

When I woke up and saw her message, my chest got heavy. Out of all people, I never expected Nia to come at me like that.

Yeah, I told my wife, "I'll think about it." But that wasn't a weakness, it was a strategy. My household wasn't hers to judge. Nia and I had always promised no judgment, that we could be real without tearing each other down. And yet here she was, calling me out like I was soft.

It burned. Because she didn't see the tightrope I was walking every damn day, balancing my marriage, my business, and her. She didn't know how much energy it took just to keep everything from blowing up.

So when she called, all sweet, acting like nothing happened, I couldn't fake it.

Nia: "So, you weren't gonna call me today?"

Malik: "Nope."

I could see her blink at the bluntness.

Nia: "Excuse me?"

Malik: "That text you sent me was disrespectful. You don't know the dynamic in my household. Since when did you start judging me?"

Her face fell. But I had to say it.

Malik: "I let you in on everything, Nia. I don't hide from you. But don't ever come at me like I'm weak. That's not who I am."

I wasn't angry, I was hurt. The woman who claimed to understand me most was now questioning the way I moved in my own home.

Nia's Voice:

His words silenced me. Because I wasn't trying to call him weak. I just wanted him to stand up, to claim his ground. But clearly, I'd struck a nerve.

I decided if Malik wasn't going to make me feel appreciated, I'd do it myself. I started eyeing this beautiful Movado chain with a black heart pendant. When I mentioned it enough, he finally got it for me, but it felt like pity more than love.

When I showed my mom, glowing, she only said:

Mom: "Oh wow, so you get a chain, and she gets a watch?"

And just like that, I shrank. Like I was lesser.

It took a week before we found our way back to our rhythm. We laughed again, talked like always. But a piece of me never forgot. The Movado wasn't just a watch anymore. It was a reminder of where I stood in his world.

23

I LOVED YOU LOUDER THAN I LOVED MYSELF

You already know how I feel when it comes to you.

These low-vibrational actions I've been moving with? They're because I put you before me.

And now that I've sat with that realization? I'm all over the fucking place.

Because deep down, I know our situation will never change, not because of me, but because you already made your decision.

And I feel stupid like a wide-eyed little girl, smitten and naive.

But the crazy part is I'm a grown-ass woman. A woman who would look any man in the face and say: "I've already found my soulmate."

Meanwhile, if it were up to you? I'd probably die before you ever said the same.

I'm not trying to be an asshole. But I've been watching. Listening.

And your actions? They don't match your words. Not even a little bit.

You're not choosing me.

You've never chosen me.

I'm not your priority. And you don't even hide it anymore.

That 80/20 video I sent? It wasn't shade. It was the truth. It's exactly what the fuck you're doing.

You've been with her longer, sure. But by your own words, I bring you more. I'm the 80. She's 20.

And yet... you're cool with watching me walk away. Cool with another man holding what was always yours.

That part right there? That's the punch in the chest. That's what breaks me.

Because you say I'm your soulmate, but you're willing to let me go love someone else because it's easier than facing your own truth.

Like I said... we are each other's karma.

And now?

Hahaha, egg on my fucking face.

Imagine giving your entire heart to your soulmate, only for them to hand it to someone else.

So yeah... that's how I woke up. Heart heavy, soul louder than ever, and that's exactly what I sent Malik.

Because sometimes, you have to hold the mirror up, even if it burns both your hands to do it. You have to see yourself as the real you and ask, "Why am I allowing this?"

I realized... if it's not good for me, if it's draining me, if it's making me forget who the hell I am then I have to stop.

And this time? I did something different. Something hard. Something overdue.

I chose myself.

I didn't pick myself halfway. I didn't whisper it in the background. I chose myself out loud.

Clear. Certain. Even through the heartbreak.

Because loving someone more than you love yourself? That's not romantic, it's self-destruction dressed in desire. And I've danced in that fire long enough.

I made the conscious decision that, in order to protect my heart,

I had to let our situation go.

And it hurt like hell.

Like cry-when-the-wind-blows kind of hurt.

Like everything-brings-tears kind of hurt.

Like unstable, rocking-in-place type grief.

But my sister, Rhea...

God, I love her.

She came through like a damn warrior.

Picked me up when I couldn't lift my own name.

Looked me dead in the eyes and reminded me

"You're stronger than you think. Stronger than this."

And that? That was the moment.

The moment I started climbing out of that emotional grave.

Crying, yes.

But crawling back to me piece by piece.

Nia: That's how I ended it with Malik...

Rhea: Maintaining.

Nia: Yeah... that's all we can do at times ■(╚⁶■

Rhea: Wow.

Nia: Yeah... Do you think I sounded like an asshole?

Rhea: Did your therapist's question help you come to this conclusion?

Nia: Yea.

Rhea: No, not at all. It was pretty straightforward. I can feel the frustration in your words.

Rhea: Honesty? Excellent.

Nia: I had convinced myself that I had found the one.

My soulmate. My best friend.

Someone I could talk to about anything, laugh with, and feel completely free with.

Someone who accepts me as I am.

Someone I could wear a damn dress for. No more "pants-wearing" Nia.

Someone who made me feel whole.

Like I was enough.

And the wild part?

I only feel that 30% of the time in a 24-hour day.

Because this same man told me, straight up, that he's not leaving his wife.

His situation is permanent.

Yet somehow, I'm the woman who "meets his needs."

He says I'm 98% of what he wants in a woman.

So why am I still here, holding on to my 30%?

That's where the low vibration comes in.

Because I haven't been ready to let go.

Because I'm tired of being lonely.

Because I've convinced myself that 30% is better than 0%.

But if a friend came to me, telling me they were living this?

I'd have questions.

I'd repeat their words back to them, so that they could hear the truth in what they're saying.

My low vibration... it comes from loving a man more than I love myself.

Rhea: Wow.

Rhea: I guess my vibration is extremely low, too, then, lol.

Nia: Lol. Find another word, girl...

Nia: No judgment here.

Rhea: I don't think we ever learned how to put ourselves first growing up.

But hey, better late than never.

Nia: And that's why mine's been so low...

Rhea: Makes sense.

Nia: The crazy thing is, I can put myself first. I do.

But when it comes to him... I'm still a work in progress.

Rhea: Realization is half the battle.

Nia: Thanks, Rhea. I just hope I can actually follow through. 🙆🏾‍♀️

Rhea: You will.

You're stronger than you know.

And you know your worth.

You deserve someone who gives you 100% nothing less.

Nia: Definitely... Thank you 💜

After making the conscious decision to choose myself

To stop holding on to something that was never going to change

To walk away from Malik and let him go...

I thought I'd feel lighter.

But instead?

I spiraled.

Like, bad.

I wasn't in the right head space at all.

I reached out to Rhea because I could feel myself slipping.

Nothing brought me joy.

Not music.

Not people.

Not jokes.

Not sunshine.

Everything felt... heavy.

Like I was crying on the outside or the inside, either way, I was crying.

I was emotionally raw, stripped down, barely holding it together.

That's when it hit me.

This wasn't just about missing Malik.

It was the grief of loving someone more than I loved myself... far too long.

The grief of realizing I stayed in a space that never had room for me to bloom.

But even in that darkness, I had Rhea.

And that's what made it bearable.

She was going through her own stuff with her husband. I won't unpack her business here, but we both knew pain.

We both understood what it felt like to carry silent heartbreak.

So we held space for each other.

We didn't have to explain everything.

We just got it.

No judgment. No advice. Just presence.

Two women, broken in different ways, still showing up to hold the other together.

Still finding ways to uplift one another when life was doing its absolute best to knock us down.

And sometimes?

That's what saves you.

Not the big breakthroughs.

Not the perfect therapy session.

But the quiet text that says:

"I got you."

(Conversation begins after Nia sends a photo of herself)

Nia: Me today... what do you see?

Rhea: Extreme pain. I can feel it.

Rhea: Don't harden your heart. I can see the hardness forming.

Nia: Yeah... my eyes just be watering on their own 🧏🏽‍♀️

Rhea: My therapist said that means your cup is full.

Nia: Yeah... It's something.

Nia: Hey.

Nia: I'm so fucking sad.

Rhea: Awww man, I'm so sorry

Rhea: You're not gonna hurt yourself, are you?

Nia: Not at all.

Rhea: Excellent. Just making sure.

Nia: Nah, I love me 🖤

Rhea: And your family loves you 🖤

NEVER forget that.

YOU ARE LOVED.

Rhea: Hey, how are you feeling today?

Nia: Man... my eyes are like waterfalls today.

This shit sucks.

I guess I just have to go through the process...

I'm so fucking mad at myself for going down this road with Malik.

Losing my only love... my best friend.

Father GOD, I'm asking you for strength to get through this...

Rhea: Prayers going out for you 🖤

Just know the pain won't last forever

Nia: Thank you.

Rhea: How are you feeling?

Nia: Hey.

I'm okay... not crying as much, just sad.

How are you?

Rhea: I'm okay, too. My prayers are working.

I was good this weekend.

Nia: That's what's up ■❤

Rhea: Sorry you're still sad.

Glad there are fewer tears.

When's therapy?

Nia: Tomorrow... thank you.

Glad you had a great weekend

How's work?

Rhea: It wasn't great, but I'm getting stronger.

Learning to love me 💕

Not bad. First day calling patients. Was super nervous

Nia: You got this.

... I thought they called you?

Rhea: No, that was the last job.

Nia: Oh, OK...

I'm sad.

Dreamt about him last night.

I feel empty.

Rhea: I'm sorry.

He probably visited you in your dream.

I know this must be rough.

Nia: Yeah, it was a weird one...

But we were together.

Rhea: Awwwwww.

So y'all can't even chat as friends?

Nia: No.

Too far gone.

Rhea: What does that mean?

Nia: Hard to casually talk to him when I want more.

Rhea: Understandable.

Nia: It'll pass. I just have to keep myself occupied.

Rhea: True. And listen to upbeat music or comedy, keep the energy up.

Nia: Thanks, sis.

Nia shared a text Malik sent after days of silence... despite her being the one who asked for the breakup.

Malik: You know damn well, deep down in your heart, that both of us are hurting. Giving you the space you wanted was the hardest thing for me to do. I didn't realize that until you asked me to do it.

I know you're working on yourself, and I've always told you I'm here for you no matter what.

Well, I meant that, even at the cost of my own feelings.

But I'm not going to be the punching bag anymore.

I'm not going to help you do low-level activities when you're meant for more.

I'm not upset. I'm just doing what needs to be done so we can move on.

And that means removing myself.

I'm not the best at expressing myself through text, but this was the best I could do without a phone call.

I gave my sister your number, just in case of an emergency.

I told her who you are and what you mean to me.

She said, "Wow, you really love her, huh?"

I stayed silent for a second and said, "In ways she may never understand."

Our love, Nia...

To the moon and back.

Nia: He wrote that...

Rhea: Woooooow.

How does that make you feel?

Nia: I'm so fucking sad.

I don't even know how I feel.

Rhea: Did you respond?

Nia: I'm just sad... depressed.

I feel empty.

Like something's missing.

I didn't respond...

Rhea: That took strength you didn't even know you had.

Good thing you have therapy tomorrow.

Nia: Yeah... I'm sad

Rhea: You did the right thing.

His message was nice, but his words still don't match his actions.

Nia: Yeah...

Even though I asked for the breakup... the silence afterwards was deafening. It was like he didn't even fight. Like he was unbothered.

Nia: My feelings are all over the place, Malik. I have to fight not to think about you, but I always lose that battle. The other day, I locked myself in my room and cried an ocean. It's like... am I really signing up to be second best? Do I want that for myself? And yet,

I'm so in love with you, it steals my breath. I've been snapping at people who don't even deserve it because my heart is stretched too thin. Some days, I feel like I'm losing my mind. I even almost said yes to someone else just out of habit, trying to patch one wound with another. That's the cycle I know.

But this with you? It has me unraveling.

Malik:

Nia... I had to pull over at a gas station yesterday and just cry. Sat there trying to figure out what the hell is going on with me. Hearing how much pain you're in makes it worse, because every part of me wants to rescue you. Be there for you. But I don't even know if we're built to survive this. I don't know if it will work. All I know is we're here.

I thought about doing the same thing... distracting myself with somebody new. But I can't. I won't. My heart already belongs to you. Always has. And I don't want to let another woman in.

Nia: When you say you're "trying to figure out what's up with you"... what does that even mean?

Malik: It means I thought I had my emotions under control. I thought I could keep them boxed up. But the truth slapped me in that car, I couldn't hold it in. I had to cry it out. For the first time in a long time, I felt it all.

And... I unblocked you.

So here we are.

Head first. No parachute. No logic.

Just that damn rabbit hole.

And the kind of love that's equal parts miracle and madness.

24

TWO BITES AND SADNESS

No one could ever be more disappointed in me than I am in myself. Jumping off the ledge again, heart-first, like I didn't already know how the fall ends. My birthday was coming up.

And honestly? I didn't want to spend it alone. Didn't want to plan a party. Didn't want to gather fake smiles for a group dinner I'd spend faking joy through.

I just... didn't want to try. Then Malik invited me to Jersey.

He said he had training that week, but I could come. And I went.

Even I was surprised. Shocked

I knew it was crazy. I could hear the judgment before anyone spoke.

Who keeps signing up for this kind of heartbreak?

Apparently... I do.

The heart will have you doing some wild shit.

And even though I tell people to follow their gut, I always end up following my heart.

Especially when it comes to him.

So yeah, my birthday was coming.

And this was the first time we'd actually be together for it.

He said he had a surprise planned. Wouldn't tell me the details.

And that alone had me glowing.

Because I remembered the things he'd told me about her birthdays:

The scavenger hunts. Spa days. Elaborate, thoughtful moments.

And now, he was being secretive with me, too.

So I assumed maybe, just maybe, I'd get something similar.

I got to Jersey, and everything felt normal. Our usual rhythm of talking, laughing, and wrapping up in each other's space.

He made me breakfast.

Brought it in on a tray, singing "Happy Birthday" like I was the only woman in the world.

In that moment, I felt so special.

Like... wow. He really did this for me.

Later, I slipped into my olive green birthday dress.

Gold heels. Nails to match. Hair laid? like royalty.

Because when I show up, I show out.

I was ready. Ready to be surprised.

Ready for a night that reminded me I was worth celebrating.

But instead... we stayed in.

He cooked again, vegetarian pasta.

And as grateful as I was for the effort, I couldn't ignore the quiet sadness that sat beside my plate.

Two bites in, and I was full.

Full from the starch... and the ache.

Full from dressing up for a moment that never came.

Maybe that makes me sound ungrateful.

But I'd be lying if I said I didn't feel cheated.

Not just out of a birthday dinner.

But out of the kind of love that plans.

He once told me, after a previous date night, that inviting me to Jersey for my birthday might not be a good idea because he knew how big birthdays were for me.

And then he did it anyway.

Invited me. Promised me the feeling.

But didn't deliver the magic.

I didn't say anything.

I swallowed the silence and kept the peace. Because I didn't want to ruin the night by naming the emptiness sitting in my chest.

We stayed in that hotel the entire week.

No surprises. No plans. Just... together.

And yes, being with him made me smile.

But behind every laugh was a quiet knowing:

I had placed myself in her shoes, hoping I'd be treated the same.

But I wasn't.

And maybe that's on me.

For believing he'd pour into me the way he did her.

For thinking this time would be different.

For showing up, over and over, hoping to feel chosen finally.

But instead?

I got pasta.

And two bites of sadness.

A Letter To Nia,

You showed up again with hope in your eyes and love in your hands.

You dressed up, not just your body, but your spirit too.

You packed your joy, ironed your expectations, and wrapped your heart in olive green.

You did what you always do:

You gave him the best parts of you, even when you knew deep down he wouldn't match the energy.

But I want you to know... I see you.

I see how hard it was to swallow that sadness on your birthday.

I see how you smiled through silence and tried to make the best of a moment that was never designed with you in mind.

I know you felt forgotten.

I know you felt like a placeholder dressed up as a partner.
But you're not crazy.
You're not dramatic.
You're not ungrateful.

You're just a woman who deserves more than effort wrapped in minimum.
You deserve celebration without compromise.
Surprises that feel sacred.
Love that doesn't come with a side of guilt or second place.

You deserve a heart that matches yours in rhythm and devotion.
A love that doesn't ask you to shrink so someone else can shine.
A love that sees you — really sees you — and chooses you fully, without hesitation.

I'm sorry you didn't get that.
Not this year.

But one day soon, I hope you'll wake up on your birthday feeling full.
Not from breakfast on a tray,
but from the love you've poured back into yourself.

I hope you stop shrinking to fit his schedule.
I hope you stop bending your boundaries for temporary joy.
And most of all?
I hope you remember that your worth has never been tied to how someone else shows up.

You are magic.
Even when the room is quiet.
Even when the plans fall through.
Even when he doesn't show up the way you hoped.

You're still magic.

Happy birthday, baby girl.
   Let this be the last time you celebrate in someone else's shadow.

Love,
   Nia

25

Reflection 24.5 — The Birthday That Broke the Spell

Anyone who knows me knows one thing for sure: I am a birthday person.

I treat my birthday like it's a national damn holiday, okay? I don't work, I don't stress, I don't lift a finger. I didn't work the day I was born, and I don't plan on working on the anniversary of it either. I celebrate me — always have, always will.

So when Malik told me he didn't think it was the best idea for us to spend my birthday together — because he knows how big I go — I was like, "Okay... cool." I felt a little sulky, but I didn't push it. Then he changed his mind. He decided not only should we spend the day together, but the entire week for my birthday.

That part right there?

That's when I placed myself in her shoes.

Because it was his idea.

He was acting all secretive about the plan, and I was giddy. Butterflies. I didn't know what was coming, but baby I was ready for all of it.

The morning of my birthday, he cooked me a beautiful breakfast with fruit. He walked into the room so nervous, singing me happy birthday, and I cheesed from ear to ear. I felt special. Seen. Considered.

And you know me — I prepared.

My olive-green dress, nails to match, everything laid out. I was pumped.

He got dressed too, looking handsome as ever, so in my mind there was no way we weren't leaving that room to celebrate my day.

But guess what?

We didn't leave. At all.

And I don't know how I hid it, but a sadness washed over me that I hadn't felt in years. Because it was my birthday, and from what he had told me about how he celebrates her birthday, why would I ever think mine would be anything less?

He made pasta, and I barely ate. Two bites. My stomach was too full of disappointment to make room for anything else. I even tried to take a picture outside in my fur coat like I was actually going somewhere — like I was actually being celebrated. But we didn't go anywhere. We stayed in the room. Watched movies. And I sat there hurting.

It felt like betrayal.

Not cheating betrayal, but emotional betrayal — the kind that says,

"You know me. You know what this day means. And still... you gave me less."

That's what hurt the most.

And it took me back to a birthday with Stephen. We were still living in Florida then. I had thrown him a whole surprise party one year — best friend flown out, everything. For my birthday, he told me to get dressed for dinner. We pulled up to what looked like a buffet, and I remember asking, "How did you even find this place?"

He said, "I asked two Mexicans at work where they take their wives for their birthdays."

My heart dropped straight into my heels.

I walked to the car because the place didn't match my energy, my outfit, nothing.

On the way home he found a nice Japanese restaurant, and that's where we ended up celebrating. But that moment taught me something:

It doesn't take much to think about the person you're with. To consider who they are. To plan with intention.

And for Malik — the person I would've chosen again and again — to put no real thought into my birthday after promising me a whole week... that crushed me. Deep. Quietly. Completely.

Maybe that's exactly what I needed.

Maybe that was the crack in the trance.

The moment I finally came to my senses.

Because choosing someone who doesn't choose you back?

Being present for someone who only offers you pieces?

Waiting for a man who celebrates you in private but somebody else in public?

That is a pain I don't wish on anybody.

And that's why I'm writing this book.

So someone reading it can hold a mirror up to themselves and finally say:

I deserve better.

Not kinda better.

Not "maybe one day" better.

But real, intentional, reciprocal love — the kind that doesn't shrink on your birthday or any day.

— Liz

26

THE NIGHT BEFORE I LET GO

The night before I left Jersey, I couldn't sleep.

My mind was loud buzzing, spinning, dragging me through every moment.

I'd tried to pretend that it didn't sting.

Like how we stayed in for my birthday.

Like how he told me I was his soulmate.

So in love with me, he said.

But still didn't choose me.

That shit had me spiraling again.

I lay there next to him, staring at the ceiling, heart racing. I kept thinking...

What if I just got back with my children's father?

The thought alone made my chest cave in.

Not because I wanted him.

But because that would mean I gave up.

That would mean I settled.

That I chose safety over joy. A familiar cage over unfamiliar freedom.

We're great co-parents, sure.

But we've been through too much.

Too many lies.

Too many open relationships.

Too many moments that shattered what was supposed to be sacred.

And even with all that...

Even after everything...

Stephen chose me.

Malik didn't.

And that?

That's the part I couldn't shake.

So I got up and walked to the living room in the hotel suite.

Poured myself drink after drink.

Slid deeper into the bottle until the edges of the truth felt dull enough to touch.

Then, I walked back into the bedroom.

He was asleep, breathing slow and steady.

I lay my head on his chest, right on his heart, and started crying.

Hard.

Not the cute kind.

The gasping, shaking, nose-running, soul-leaving-your-body kind.

I don't even know if I was talking to him or the universe, but it all came out.

"You chose her," I sobbed. "And he... he chose me. How does that make sense? Why do I always end up holding the short end of love?"

He stirred but didn't say anything. Maybe he didn't know what to say.

I kept crying, curling up next to him like his arms could shield me from a truth they helped build.

Eventually, I passed out.

The next morning, Malik was getting ready for work. I could feel him moving around the room, slower than usual.

He looked over and said quietly,

"Are we going to talk about what happened last night?"

I blinked.

"What do you mean?"

He raised an eyebrow.

"You don't remember?"

I didn't. Not really. The crying? The venting? My face had been buried in his shirt. It was all a blur.

"We'll talk when I go to lunch," he said, grabbing his things.

I crawled back under the covers and went straight to sleep, hoping rest might dull the ache.

When lunch came, he called.

"You were crying... on my chest," he said softly. "You needed to get that out. I let you.

You didn't even realize how much was bottled up, huh?"

I stayed quiet. Embarrassed. Numb.

But deep down... something had shifted.

That night broke me.

But it also made something crystal clear:

If I want my happy back, my goofy, belly-laughing, hair-tied, blasting-music-in-the-kitchen self, I have to let this go. Really let it go. Not halfway. Not emotionally still-there but physically gone.

All the we've tried before doesn't matter anymore.

The truth is... It's taking too much from me now.

I'm tired of crying over someone who told me flat out that he's not leaving.

Tired of loving someone who gives me just enough to stay, but not enough to thrive.

Tired of convincing myself that 30% happiness is better than none at all.

So I told him straight:

"You're not in love with me."

He went quiet.

Even got a little attitude.

But I didn't back down.

"You love me," I said. "You have feelings for me. But you're not in love with me.

Because no man in love chooses convenience over connection; no man in love lets the woman who knows his soul walk out the door without a fight."

And I meant that shit.

So yeah. This is my story.

Still healing.

Still aching.

But finally facing myself in the mirror.

And if you're reading this right now, I hope you find your strength in these words from the pieces I shattered so you don't have to.

We all deserve more.

We deserve a love that chooses us out loud.

Not in whispers. Not in moments.

Not in hotel rooms where we cry ourselves to sleep.

You are not a secret.

And if someone treats you like one,

baby run. Choose yourself even if it shakes. Even if it hurts.

Because I'm living proof;

It's not easy.

But it's possible.

And one day, you'll look back and thank yourself for walking away.

Until then?

Keep going.

Love you. Peace.

Nia

27

Reflection 26.5 — The Night I Finally Woke Up

The night after my birthday, I couldn't sleep. My mind wouldn't stop. Voices, thoughts, emotions—I was spiraling. It was like my birthday, or really the lack of celebration, snapped me out of a trance I didn't even realize I was in. Something in me woke up, and it wouldn't go back to sleep.

So there I was, drinking way more Martel than any sane cognac lover should. (If you're a cognac drinker and you don't know about Martel—baby, go find out.) I drank too much, crawled back into bed with Malik, and basically cried all over his face.

Yeah... in the book I said his chest.
   But the truth?
   His face.

And not a cute cry either. According to him, it was an ugly cry. He told me that later because I genuinely didn't remember. But what I do remember is that he lay there and let me unload. He didn't run. He didn't shut down. He didn't roll away. He just let me empty all that pain, all that confusion, all those years of loving someone I could never fully have.

And the truth spilled out:

He chose her.

Stefan chose me.

But none of it felt right.

In my heart of hearts, I thought Malik and I were meant to be. I told myself our re connection after twelve years meant it was our time. That everything we'd survived, every silence, every text, every moment—was leading us back to each other.

But that was my belief.

Not his.

Malik didn't feel that way.

And loneliness can trick you. It can make old love look brand new. It can make familiar feel like destiny. With Stephen, there was always love—deep love. He loved me hard. But so much had happened between us that I didn't feel the same anymore. I love him, absolutely. I don't wish him anything but the best. But I don't love him the way he loves me. And realizing that I might end up back with him—not because of passion or purpose, but because it was familiar—broke me.

The thought gutted me.

It brought me to my knees.

Because settling in love?

That's something I was never built to do.

I would rather be alone, traveling the world, embracing my peace, than be in a relationship where my heart isn't alive. I believe none of us were put here to settle. We deserve to be loved fully, not conveniently.

And that's what sent me into that rabbit hole. The truth hit me: Malik is ten toes down in his marriage. He is not leaving. Not now, not later. Not for the love story I imagined we could finally have.

At some point that night, I blacked out. Happens when I drink too much. The next day when he said, "Are we going to talk about last night?" I was confused. There's a piece of the night missing—just blank. I remember going to the living room. I don't remember returning to the bedroom. But he filled in the gaps.

It is what it is.

I don't agree with his decisions. He doesn't agree with mine.
   Different opinions.
   Different realities.
   Yet here we were, tied together in a story that was never going to end the way I once hoped.

And that's when it became clear:
   Writing this book wasn't just storytelling.
   It was a release.
   A way to choose myself.

Because despite the amount of love I have for Malik, I know—deep in my bones—that someone exists who will love me with that same intensity, if not more. Someone who will choose me without hesitation. Without excuses. Without needing a split life or shared loyalty.

Maybe Malik came into my life to show me what real love feels like—or maybe he didn't. Because if it were real-real...the kind that's mutual and destined... we'd be together right now.

But we're not.

Right now, I'm living alone. I'm being a boss. Running my salon. Running my lounge. Still traveling, still exploring. Still discovering who Liz is outside of anyone else's shadow.

And I know—truly know—that my Mr. Right will find me. I'll bump into him somewhere in this big world. A man who chooses me without blinking. A man whose love doesn't ask me to shrink, wait, sacrifice, or survive.

One day, he's going to walk into my life and make everything make sense.

Until then, I hold on to this truth:
  We were not placed here to be loveless.
  We were not placed here to settle.
  We all deserve a love that pours back into us—not one that only quenches someone else's thirst.

Thank you for reading.
  Love y'all.
  —Liz

28

MALIK'S RESPONSE TO THE READERS

"So I know y'all probably wondering... with me being married, why even go down this road with Nia?

Truth is, I asked myself the same damn thing more times than I can count.

It started with a question. Simple, but heavy:

'Will you be in this open relationship with me?'

At first, I froze. Like... wait, did she really just ask that?

Not in a disrespectful way, but in a 'this is Nia' way. The woman I'd admired for years.

The way she walked into a room was confidence without effort. The way she smiles when nervous, the tilt of her head when deep in thought. There was always something about her. Always.

I had a crush on her long before I even knew what to do with those feelings.

But when she asked... it wasn't just about attraction. It was about connection. About trust. About her finally opening a door she had always kept shut.

At first, I said no. Not because I didn't want to say yes, God knows I did, but because I was scared. Scared of what it meant, scared of the weight it carried.

I was married. She knew that. I knew that. We weren't supposed to go there.

But she asked. And the way she asked it wasn't out of lust.

It was out of loneliness. Out of survival. Out of needing something real.

And it hit me... she didn't need me to fix her. She needed me to see her, to show up for her in a way no one else ever had.

So yeah, I called her back. I said yes. Not because I was reckless, but because I knew what we had was rare. Messy? Yeah. Complicated? Absolutely. But real. Realer than anything I'd felt in a long time.

So to answer your question... "Why did I go down that road with Nia?

Because sometimes the heart moves before the head can catch up. And when you love someone, truly love someone, you don't always take the path that makes sense. You take the one that makes you feel alive."

On Reconnecting After 12 Years

"Knowing I wasn't leaving my marriage, why did I reconnect with Nia after twelve long years?

Wow... that's a heavy question. Where do I start?

When Nia called to say she was coming to Orlando, I was already in a dark place, grappling with my marriage. Correction: I was fighting for my marriage while trying to make sense of everything else. Financial insecurity, diminished self-worth, marital turmoil, and the weight of finding my purpose all seemed to crescendo at once.

Then I got her call.

Her announcement felt surreal, like a flicker of hope trying to pierce the gloom surrounding me. I could hear the excitement in her voice, and despite my doubts, it ignited something inside me. My heart raced, skipping a beat or two as I wondered if this was real or just another fleeting dream. When she finally told me she'd arrived in Orlando, a rush of adrenaline washed over me, momentarily eclipsing all my worries."

As I went out to meet her, anticipation thrummed through my veins. I knocked on the door and when she opened it, the weight of the world seemed to lift. In that moment, everything that made sense and what didn't faded away. The struggles I had been enduring paled in comparison to the warmth radiating from her presence. The darkness of my circumstances felt less daunting, as though Nia's arrival carried a glimmer of light, an invitation to reconnect with joy, hope, and perhaps even clarity.

In that instant, the chaos of my life ebbed, replaced by a profound connection that reminded me of the beauty of companionship and the potential for renewal. It was a turning point, a reminder that even in our darkest times, the light of friendship can guide us back to ourselves.

"Malik, help us understand... If you're not in love with your wife, and you say you love Nia with everything in you, then why stay? What keeps you rooted in a life that no longer fills you, while reaching for a woman who does? Fear? Guilt? Or is it that loving her costs more than you're willing to pay?"

Malik:

"From the beginning, we met each other already tied to someone else. Nia had her relationship, I had mine. When we crossed that line, we both knew the situation, and we were okay with it.

At the end of the day, we went back to our partners. That was our normal. We let each other live in those relationships while still making space for us.

Years passed, and I was still in my relationship when we found our way back to each other. Again, Nia knew my situation, and I thought I knew hers. That was just how we operated, she let me be in my marriage, and also be with her. And I got used to that.

Over time, the feelings got deeper. We became 100% locked in emotionally, and I never hid how I felt. I was honest with her about where I stood. I was in my marriage, and I still wanted to be with Nia.

That's what I meant when I said, 'She let me.' She let me exist in both worlds, and we lived in that truth for years."

WHAT NIA HEARD:

He never lied to me.
He told me he loved me.
And he told me he wasn't leaving his marriage.

PERIOD.

I was the fool who turned "never" into "maybe."
The one who loved him like he was mine when he was never going to be.
The one who kept pouring a thousand percent into someone giving me thirty.

That's not love.
That's self-betrayal.

He told me over and over that he's not going anywhere.
So, if I'm still here?
THAT. IS. ON. ME.

Dead ends don't turn into doorways.
Stop waiting.
Stop begging.
Stop bleeding for someone who won't meet you halfway.

Take your love back.
Pour it into yourself.
And don't you ever give it away again until it's to someone free to love you back.

Someone who will climb the highest mountain,
scream your name into the wind,
and let the whole damn universe know
the love they have for you.

If you're reading this...
and you're the one who's always waiting,
always understanding,
always hoping they'll choose you eventually...

Stop.

Because you deserve a love that doesn't almost.
   A love that doesn't hide.
   A love that doesn't hurt more than it heals.

They say love is patient,
   but that doesn't mean you have to be.

You don't have to keep auditioning
   for a role they're too scared to cast you in.

Choose yourself.
   Even if your voice shakes.
   Even if your bed feels too big at first.
   Even if your heart screams for one more chance.

Because the moment you say,
   "I'm done being almost,"
   that's the moment your healing begins.

This is your sign.
   This is your mirror.

Read it.
   Weep if you must.
   Then rise.

You are not someone's secret.
   You are the whole story.

29

Final Reflection — A Letter From Liz

To the woman reading this...

To the man reading this...

To anyone who has ever been the "in-between" in someone else's life:

Let me talk to you for real, from my heart to yours.

I didn't write this book to expose anyone.

I didn't write it for pity, sympathy, or judgment.

I wrote it because there comes a moment in life when you stop whispering your truth and start walking in it.

For years, I loved in silence.

I loved in pieces.

I loved in the shadows of someone else's choices.

And that kind of love?

It chips at you.

It steals from you.

It convinces you to accept crumbs and call them meals, moments and call them memories, pain and call it passion.

But here's the truth I had to face:

Love is not supposed to hurt more than it heals.

Love is not supposed to make you feel replaceable.

Love is not supposed to require you to shrink so someone else can stay comfortable.

I stayed too long.

I loved too hard.

I believed too deeply.

But I also learned.

I learned what it means to pour into someone who can't pour back.

I learned how loneliness can dress itself up as "connection."

I learned how familiarity can trick you into thinking it's destiny.

And I learned — the hard way — that choosing someone who won't choose you is the slowest heartbreak you'll ever survive.

So if you're reading this and you are the "in-between"...

The secret love...

The emotional backup...

The safe place someone runs to but will never stand beside...

Let me tell you what I wish someone had told me sooner:

You are not a temporary space.

You are not a convenience.

You are not an escape route.

You are not the quiet corner someone comes to rest in while living loudly with someone else.

You deserve to be chosen without hesitation.

You deserve a love that stands ten toes down on your name.

You deserve someone who is sure about you, proud of you, and willing to build with you in the daylight — not borrow you in the dark.

And if walking away feels impossible...
If the thought of letting go feels like losing oxygen...
Trust me when I say this:

Your future will not fall apart because one person couldn't rise to match your heart.

Please hear me:
You are allowed to let go of what is killing you.
You are allowed to stop fighting for someone who would never fight for you.
You are allowed to choose yourself — loudly, unapologetically, fully.

Choosing myself saved my life.
Not because it was easy, but because it was necessary.
Because at some point, I had to stop begging love to see me and start seeing myself.

And the moment I did?
My healing started.
My power returned.
My peace came home.

This book is not a tragedy.
It's a resurrection.
It's the story of a woman who finally remembered who she was.

And if you are anywhere in that journey — beginning, middle, or end — please know this:

You are worthy of real love.

You are worthy of being chosen.

You are worthy of a love that doesn't make you wait, wonder, or weep.

I pray that reading my truth helps you speak yours.

I pray it reminds you that you're not alone.

I pray you find the courage to release what is not for you — and make room for what is.

I love you for taking this journey with me.

I love you for seeing me.

And I hope this book helps you see yourself a little more clearly too.

With strength,

With honesty,

With a healed heart,

— Liz

30

Conclusion

The Other Side of Healing

Loving someone who sleeps next to another will change you.

It will stretch your heart in ways you didn't know were possible and test the limits of your self-worth.

You'll learn what it means to hold on to something that was never fully yours,

and then, what it means to finally let go.

Healing doesn't happen in a straight line.

Some days you'll feel brand new—light, unbothered, free.

Other days, a song, a scent, or a random memory will pull you right back into the ache.

Don't fight it. Feel it.

Every tear, every pause, every moment of silence is proof that you cared deeply.

It's proof that your love was real, even if it wasn't returned the way you deserved.

But there will come a day when you'll wake up and the thought of them won't sting anymore.

You'll realize that closure didn't come from their apology—it came from your growth.

You'll look in the mirror and see someone stronger, wiser, softer, but no longer broken.

This is your reminder: healing takes time.

Don't rush the process.

Keep moving forward—one breath, one boundary, one sunrise at a time.

Because the other side of the bed might be empty for now,

but the other side of healing?

That's where peace lives.

That's where you live.

Epilogue

This is no fairy tale, and I'm not the girl who got the guy.

So to be in love with someone who says they're in love with you but still goes home to somebody else? That's a pain with no warning label. It's slow. Sick. Stealthy. You fight a war by yourself, trying to prove your worth to someone who has already made their choice and it's not you.

Once that person tells you they're not leaving their relationship, their marriage, believe them. I don't care how many times they say they're in love with you, or how good it feels when you're together. The truth is, the only way this ends is when YOU end it.

And yes, your heart will break.

Yes, it will damn near take you out.

Yes, you'll cry until your eyes are swollen shut.

But baby... You gotta get out.

I wouldn't wish this kind of love on anybody. The highs when you hear their voice, the lows when they say they've got to go. It's like being addicted to your own heartbreak, a junkie for moments that aren't even real.

And I get it, it's hard to walk away. It's hard to stop answering when your whole body still aches for them. But let me be real: the longer you stay, the deeper the wound. The uglier the healing.

I had a dream once.

Leah and I was each standing on separate volcanoes. Malik had to choose who lives and who burns.

And your girl? I burned to. A. Crisp.

Tears in my eyes, chest wide open, heart scattered all over the damn place. And they just walked away... hand in hand.

While I stood there, melting in the fire like some sad, love-struck fool.

But here's the kicker...- He never lied to me. Never fed me half-truth. He told me exactly what it was. And I still stayed.

I can't even blame him. I gotta hold that "L".

So if you're reading this, whoever you are, choose you.

Because the one that's meant for you?

They won't come with a side of confusion.

They won't belong to someone else.

Put yourself first even if it breaks you.

Date yourself. Love yourself. Cry when you need to.

And when you're ready? Book that solo trip. Get your passport.

Because the one that's really for you?

They might be out there somewhere, waiting for you to show up whole.

I say this with every piece of my healing heart.

If they're not choosing you... Stop choosing them.

Chuck the damn deuces. 🫧⬛💋

"I didn't leave because I wanted to, I left because staying started to cost me parts of myself I couldn't afford to lose. And loving him should've never meant abandoning me."

Afterword

From Liz, With Love

Writing this book was more than storytelling—
  it was soul work.

Every chapter pulled pieces of me I thought I'd buried.
  Every memory I tried to forget found its way back through the pen.
  And somewhere between the pain, the laughter, and the lessons,
  I realized this wasn't just Nia's story—
  it was mine.
  And maybe, it's yours too.

If you've ever loved someone who wasn't fully yours,
  if you've ever prayed for a different ending,
  if you've ever stayed hoping love could rewrite its own rules—
  I see you.

And I want you to know:
  you are not weak for loving deeply.
  You are human.
  You gave your best with the tools and the heart you had at the time.

But there comes a moment when you must choose
  peace over patterns,
  clarity over confusion,
  and yourself over someone else's comfort.

Healing doesn't happen overnight.
   Some days it will feel like freedom.
   Other days it will feel like loss.
   But every day, it will lead you closer to you.

So, take your time.
   Feel it all.
   And when you rise—because you will rise—
   let it be in full color,
   full power,
   and full truth.

You are not defined by the love that didn't last.
   You are defined by the courage it took to walk away.

Thank you for walking with me through these pages,
   for holding space for my truth,
   and for finding your own strength
   in between the lines.

May your next chapter be softer.
   May it be lighter.
   May it finally be yours.

With love,
   Liz

About the Author

Elizabeth "Liz" Williams is a Houston-based storyteller, restaurateur, and beauty entrepreneur who believes healing is a daily practice and community is a love language. She founded Xquisite Vybz—an island-inspired lounge and kitchen—and Xquisite Natural Hair Care, a salon devoted to protective styles and healthy hair. In both spaces, Liz leads with generosity, creativity, and conversation.

Her debut book, The Other Side of the Bed: Loving Someone Who Sleeps Next to Another, spans more than twenty years of complicated love. Through vivid scenes, humor, and hard truths, Liz explores longing, loyalty, boundaries, and the moment a woman decides to choose herself. It's a mirror and a map—for anyone who's ever stayed too long, loved too hard, and finally learned to let go.

When she isn't writing or curating island-inspired flavors, she's pouring her love into her greatest creations—her children.

Dedicated to my beautiful babies:

Heavenly Giovanni, Dominic, and Taliya —
each of you are the rhythm behind my strength,
the reason I rise, and the light that keeps my spirit shining.

Forever, Mommy loves you.

You can connect with me on:

🌐 https://www.instagram.com/LizLovingLife_1978

🔗 https://www.instagram.com/XquisiteNaturallyByLiz

🔗 https://www.instagram.com/XquisiteVybzLLC

www.ingramcontent.com/pod-product-compliance
Lightning Source LLC
Chambersburg PA
CBHW020154120726
47903CB00007B/2556

* 9 7 9 8 9 9 4 0 0 9 1 0 9 *